Very SERIOUS Children

by Caroline Adderson

illustrations by Joe Weissmann

Scholastic ... Ltd.
Toronto New Y... ... Auckland Sydney
Mexico City New Delhi Hong Kong Buenos Aires

Scholastic Canada Ltd.
604 King Street West, Toronto, Ontario M5V 1E1, Canada

Scholastic Inc.
557 Broadway, New York, NY 10012, USA

Scholastic Australia Pty Limited
PO Box 579, Gosford, NSW 2250, Australia

Scholastic New Zealand Limited
Private Bag 94407, Greenmount, Auckland, New Zealand

Scholastic Children's Books
Euston House, 24 Eversholt Street, London NW1 1DB, UK

Library and Archives Canada Cataloguing in Publication
Adderson, Caroline, 1963-
Very serious children / Caroline Adderson ; illustrations by Joe
Weissmann.
ISBN 978-0-439-93751-1
I. Weissmann, Joe, 1947- II. Title.
PS8551.D3267V47 2007   jC813'.54   C2007-901042-3

0-439-93751-5

6 5 4 3 2 1   Printed in Canada   07 08 09 10 11

This paper used in this book is 100% free of ancient forest fibre
and contains 30% post-consumer recycled pulp.

Contents

For Patrick, my not-too-serious child.
                                                      — C.A.

Me — Nicky H.H. Grant

Nicky's not short for Nicholas, though you probably thought it was. I'll tell you what it's short for —
but if you're the kind of person who makes fun of
kids with weird names, I'd rather you closed this
book right now. Just stop reading. Leave it on the
bus or a park bench for a nicer kid to pick up.
Unless you got it from the library, of course.

It's Nickelodeon.

You probably know that Nickelodeon is a TV
channel that plays cartoons all day. But a long
long time ago, before TV, a nickelodeon was a
movie theatre that charged a nickel to get in. I
read that in the dictionary.

There. Now you know. My name means "cheap
movie theatre."

That's not all. You're probably wondering what
the H.H. stands for in Nicky H.H. Grant. I may as
well tell you: Ha Ha.

1

Go ahead. Laugh all you want. At least my name shortens to a normal name, but what about my poor little brother, Saggy? Saggy comes from his initials: S.A.G. Grant.

Guess. Just try to guess what that stands for.

Split A Gut.

I'm not kidding.

We asked them. We said, "Mom? Dad? Why did you give us these weird names?"

They said, "Because when you were born we could tell that you were both Very Serious Children."

"How could you tell?" we asked.

"Because you were crying."

They hoped our names would cheer us up.

Mr. and Ms Toots

"Your mom and dad? They mean well." That's what Mr. Fudge kept telling us. "They're happy people and they want everyone else to be happy too."

Before I tell you about our parents, I have to issue a caveat. A ca-vee-at, in case you don't know, is a warning. During every performance of Mr. Fudge's Fantastic Flyers, he would announce, "Ladies and gentlemen, a caveat!" This was just before the cannon shot my dad into the stands.

"The management is not responsible for injuries sustained due to impact with the flying clown!"

This is my caveat: If you're the kind of kid who's always dreamed of running away to join the circus, stop reading. Give this book to a sensible friend. Well, you can read the next chapter called "How We Lived," but stop there. I don't want to be the one to spoil your dreams.

Our mom and dad are clowns. When they're performing, they go by the names Mr. and Ms Toots. They wear make-up, but their hair is real. I mean, it's really that colour. "It's natural!" Mom says. Their noses are foam balls. There's a slit in the ball and you stuff your nose inside it. It doesn't smell very good. Also for your information: their feet aren't really that big.

When they're not performing, when they're Mr. and Mrs. Grant, my parents still seem like clowns. My mom wears dresses with big polka dots and my dad always sports a bow tie. They share socks. Striped ones, of course. Even if they wore jeans and T-shirts and plain socks like ordinary parents, I bet people would still guess what kind of work they did.

Saggy just came into my room (I have my own room now!) to ask what I'm doing. I told him, "I'm writing the story of our lives so far."

"Does it have a happy ending?" he asked.

"So far it does," I told him. "Of course, we're not at the end yet. But I have a good feeling."

"What part are you writing now?"

"I'm just telling how Mom and Dad are real clowns, not just people dressed up as clowns."

"Tell them about their wedding rings."

"Okay. Now get lost."

Unlike most married people, they wear their wedding rings on their right hands. "Because we're so right for each other," says Dad. That's not all. When you shake hands with them, the rings buzz and give off a tingly shock. Everyone is very surprised the first time, and no one shakes hands with them twice.

How We Lived

I should tell you that I'm writing this on a typewriter, if you can believe it. We found it in the attic. A typewriter is a machine from a long, long time ago, back when they used to have nickelodeons. It's threaded with a ribbon soaked in ink. When the typewriter key smacks the ribbon, the letter prints on the page. I don't know what I'm going to do if the ribbon dries out. It's pretty faint already. So if you turn the page in the middle of a sentence and there's nothing after that, you'll know the reason. It won't be because I got lazy and didn't want to finish the story!

Back in the time of nickelodeons and typewriters, more people went to the circus. They didn't have TVs and computers and other modern kinds of entertainment, so when the circus came to town, it was a big event. The travelling circuses were different in the olden days. Back then, animals performed. There were dancing bears and elephants balancing on balls and tigers that leaped through flaming hoops. Then the SPCA said it was cruel. I have to say I agree. I'm glad that the circus has changed.

Mr. Fudge has been in the business for most of his life. He was full of stories about his "animal relatives," as he liked to call them, and his camper walls were crowded with pictures from the early days. In one, Mr. Fudge posed with a bear in a tutu. I felt sorry for the bear. (How would you like to wear a dress?) In another, a lion sat on Mr. Fudge's chest while he fed it an ice cream cone. He said that lions prefer strawberry. I don't think lions are meant to eat ice cream at all, or live in cages. They should be free. When I told Mr. Fudge this, he said, "You're right, Nicky, of course. But those days? Those were the days!"

We only had two animals in our circus: Mr. Fudge's white rabbit, Sir John A. Macdonald, and our Coco. Coco is a chihuahua, a small, difficult-to-spell dog with bulgy eyes.

People sometimes ask us if her collar is too tight. It's not. That's just how she looks. I wish we could set Coco free, but she'd only come back.

Also working in the olden-days circuses were people with unfortunate health problems. They had to put on costumes and sit in cages under embarrassing signs like THE BEARDED LADY or THE FATTEST WOMAN ON EARTH or TOM THUMB. Mr. Fudge had pictures of these "relatives" too. One was Sal-Sally. Sometimes Mr. Fudge would lock himself in his camper for hours, crying, "Just make up your mind! I'm begging you!" Saggy and I would peek in the window and see him talking to the picture of Sal-Sally he kept by his bed. I thought he was asking her to make up her mind whether she was a man or a woman, because in the picture she wore a skirt on one leg and pants on the other. She had long hair on the skirt side, and short hair and a beard on the pants side.

"That's not it," Mom told me. "He's been asking Sal-Sally to marry him for years. He won't say yes and she won't say no."

We didn't make fun of any people in our circus. One time we did put Grandma Jack in a tent and charge a dollar to see her, but it wasn't because of her size. If we had been that kind of circus, Saggy and I would probably have had to sit in a cage under the sign VERY SERIOUS CHILDREN. Saggy and I didn't perform, though of course we know lots of tricks from having been born into a circus. The Fantastic Flyers were basically a few acrobats plus Mr. and Ms Toots, Coco, Bruce the Strongish Man, and Mr. Fudge — who did magic tricks as well as being the impresario. (That's an Italian word that sounds better than master of ceremonies.) Grandma Jack sold tickets, popcorn and candy floss. Sometimes a fire breather joined up, or a sword swallower. For a few weeks last summer we had the Lees.

Every year we followed spring, heading north from a town in Texas called Canadian, where we spent the winter in a mobile home park. We would tour through Oklahoma and Kansas, Nebraska and the Dakotas, then over the border into

Canada for our summer tour of the prairie provinces — Manitoba, Saskatchewan and Alberta. Every week we would stop in a new town. Mr. Fudge said prairie people, Canadian or American, were the last great circus-goers. He said they didn't know *how* to boo. Come fall, we would cross the border again and head south once more. The year before last, though, Mr. Fudge didn't stop to put on shows on the way back. He said people didn't seem as friendly any more, but Mom and Dad thought it was really that Mr. Fudge was tired. He's seventy-eight years old.

We had our own little camper. These days, if you pass through our town in Saskatchewan, you'll know our house right away because it's the last one before the wheat begins, and you can see the camper in the backyard. Glued all over it are plastic animals and toys and mirrors, what Grandma Jack called "gewgaws." Most of them come from Pink Pelican Popcorn, though we bought a souvenir in every town we performed in and glued all those on too.

Inside the camper there was barely enough room to swing a chihuahua. I know this for a fact because once, for fun, Mom and Dad took Coco by the back legs and tested the expression out. Coco usually rode on the dashboard, under a pine-tree-shaped air freshener hanging from the rear-view mirror. (We got the air freshener because of the Coco smell.) At night she slept on the dashboard too, while Saggy and I shared the bunk above the bench that opened out into Mom and Dad's bed. We ate at a small table that folded up to make room for the bed. There was a tiny stove to cook on and a miniature fridge. We had to wash ourselves and the dishes in the same little sink. (Though not at the same time!) Now and then we went to camp-

grounds and paid to use the showers. On hot days the whole circus would stop at a lake and jump in to get clean.

The few cupboards we had were so crammed, mostly with costumes, that we had to warn each other when we were about to open one. "Ladies and gentlemen! The management is not responsible for injuries sustained due to impact with the flying stuff!" Then, like a Jack-in-the-box, shoes and wigs and ruffled collars would burst out.

Life wasn't so bad, I guess, except for all the driving. You see, I get carsick.

.

Where Are We, Anyway?

Maybe you've always wanted to go on a trip in a camper. Maybe you think it would be really fun. But you've probably never thought of the hours and hours of driving, when you have to sit at the table with your seat belt on. You can't draw because the table is vibrating. You can't play chess because the pieces fall off the board every time you hit a pothole. If you're like me, you can't even read, because you'd throw up for sure.

The prairie isn't actually all that flat. There are many interesting landforms to look at, if you have nothing better to do than stare out the window. And don't forget the famous prairie sky! One of Saggy's and my favourite games was "Circus Clouds." Whoever saw the most elephants and top hats and juggling balls won. The only circus shape we didn't count was candy floss. It wasn't enough of a challenge.

Ours was always the last camper in the entourage. I can't begin to tell you how many times we got lost. Usually we took a wrong turn without realizing it. Or the engine broke down. Or whoever had the map — Mom or Dad — had been holding it upside down all along.

Once we got stuck behind a slow-moving pick-up truck with a big sign. Its lights were flashing and for an hour our whole windshield was filled with two big words:

WIDE LOAD

It was all I could see, and it made me queasy.

"Honk the horn, Red," said Dad, who was driving. Mom took the toy horn out of the glove compartment, unrolled the window, and squeezed the rubber bulb. It wasn't loud enough.

"Pass him, Dad," I pleaded. "I'm getting sick looking at that sign."

"What does it say?" Saggy asked.

"Wide Load," I told him.

"What's wide about it?" Saggy asked, and he was right. It was just an ordinary truck.

"As you pass him, Len," said Mom, "drive

along beside him so I can tell him that his sign is wrong."

"That's nice of you, Red. Children? See what a considerate mother you have?"

Dad checked that the oncoming lane was clear, then stepped on the gas and drew up alongside the truck. Mom honked the horn frantically. The driver noticed and unrolled the window. "Your sign is wrong!" Mom shouted to him.

"What?" the driver shouted back.

"Your sign! It's incorrect!" To Dad she said, "Drive on, Len. He'll realize it himself when he stops."

As soon as we managed to pull in front of the pickup truck, it began to honk. Dad was impressed. "Now that's what I call a horn," he said.

Saggy and I gaped. "Look!"

Up ahead was a much bigger truck, towing a trailer with a house on it. An actual house. Yellow with blue trim. The pickup behind us kept honking. "He wants you to get out of the way, Dad," I said.

Dad pulled to the side of the road and stopped. The pickup passed us and caught up to the trailer. For a long time we watched the house getting smaller in the distance. It was such a strange sight, like something you'd see in a dream — a house travelling down a road. When it was far enough away to be a dollhouse, Mom sighed. "Wouldn't that be the way to go?" She was probably thinking of all the extra cupboard space.

Then Dad made his usual suggestion. "Why don't we get out and stretch?"

This was what we always did when we got lost. We got out and stretched, and then waited for someone to come and find us.

Mom jumped the ditch and tamped flat a patch of winter wheat. "Everybody? Ready? Touch your toes!"

We all touched our toes, except Coco, who chased her tail.

"Good! Now reach! Reach out! Touch somebody else's toes!"

No one came to get us while we were stretching, so Dad waded back to the camper for the maps. He handed them out and we spread them on our laps. "Where are we, anyway?"

"Minnesota," Mom said, because that was the map she had.

"Nonsense. It says Alberta right here." Dad shook his map at Mom.

She flapped hers at him. "Minnesota! Can't you read?"

They love to pretend to argue.

"What does mine say?" Saggy asked.

"Saskatchewan," I told him. "But we're in Manitoba now."

Dad said, "Let's all look and see if we can find a town that sounds familiar."

"Eyebrow," Mom read.

"Elbow," I read off Saggy's map.

"Entwistle," Dad read.

"Fairlight."

"Welldone."

"Goodeve."

Mom read, "Caroline," and then we looked for towns with women's names — Irma, Rosemary, Hilda, Mildred. We looked for towns with men's names — Herbert, Bruno, Douglas, Plato. We looked for towns with animal names — Porcupine Hills, Swan Plain, Moose Jaw, Fox Valley, Turtle Mountain, Rabbit Lake . . .

"Rabbits can't swim," Saggy pointed out.

Coco yipped. She wanted a town named after her too.

"Lookie here," said Dad. "There's a town called Limerick."

And so we spent the rest of the time trying to make up limericks using the names of the towns.

"There was a young Viking from Plenty . . ."

"A Cadillac driving through Outlook . . ."

Saggy got bored by all the wordplay and started to cry. Just then Bruce the Strongish Man's camper pulled up in front of ours at the side of the road. The outside is painted with a picture of Bruce holding up the world. The real Bruce looks just like it — so inflated with muscles, his head seems too small for his body. When he squeezed out of his camper and waved, we felt a breeze move over us. In a single stride he cleared the ditch. Then the

grasshoppers began springing all around us because, for them, Bruce's approach was an earthquake.

"Bruce!" Saggy squealed, and Bruce scooped him up and set him on his shoulder like a parrot.

"What happened?" he asked us.

"A funny thing," said Dad, folding up the maps.

As if this had never happened before, Bruce said, "Folks? How about you follow me? I'll lead."

Saggy asked to ride with Bruce. "Go ahead," Mom said.

But our camper wouldn't start! It must have thought it was finished driving for the day. Mom and Dad opened the hood and scolded the engine, but it didn't do any good.

Bruce shrugged his enormous shoulders. He handed Saggy and his keys to Mom, then got behind our camper and started to push. Even when he threw his huge bulk at it, we could see that the camper wasn't going to budge.

"Saggy," I whispered, "help him."

Saggy scrambled right up Bruce's back and perched on his shoulder again. With one nudge from his foot, the camper lurched forward. After that, Bruce was able to push it all the way to town, barehanded, with just that little bit of extra help from Saggy.

Mom drove Bruce's camper slowly behind him. She put the flashers on.

I Was Lonely

I bet you have a lot of friends. You're probably friends with the kids on your street and the kids in your class. But when you're a circus kid, you don't have a street because you live in a camper. You don't have a class because you don't go to school. You do your schoolwork by *correspondence*. Back then I would have done anything to sit in a room full of kids at a real desk and have an actual teacher teach me. Well, not *anything*. I probably wouldn't have walked the tightrope.

Mr. Fudge arranged for the Ministry of Education to send me lessons. He wrote them what towns we'd be in and when. Every few weeks I'd go down to the local post office where a big envelope addressed to Nicky H.H. Grant, General Delivery, would be waiting. General Delivery, in case you're not familiar with the term, is where you get your mail sent when you don't have a proper address. You just tell the person at the post office your name and ask if there's any mail for you and they go get it. Try it next time you go on holidays. Before you leave, send a letter to yourself.

Even more than school, I wanted a friend. I had my brother, of course, but he was my brother and only five years old. I wanted a friend my own age, someone who liked me for myself and wouldn't ask if I could swallow fire, or if I'd ever been sawed in half. Someone who wouldn't lose interest in me like so many other kids had when I told him that I was just a regular kid who happened to have clowns for parents.

Last year, when the circus was performing in Encore, Saskatchewan, I went to town to pick up my envelope. I took the unicycle. Almost as soon as I reached the main street, a boy in a baseball cap who looked about nine too (I'm ten now) came riding up beside me on his bike. "Wow," he said. "Are you with Mr. Fudge's Fantastic Flyers?"

I nodded but kept riding. The boy rode along with me. When we reached the post office, he left his bike beside the unicycle and followed me inside. "My name's Owen," he said.

"Do you have anything for Nicky H.H. Grant?" I asked the woman behind the counter.

"Nice to meet you, Nicky," Owen said.

I didn't say anything. I wasn't trying to be rude. I just knew from experience that Owen only wanted to be my friend because I was with the circus. When he saw me coming into town he didn't say to himself, "Here's a new boy. I think I'll make him feel welcome." He noticed me because I was riding a unicycle. If I'd walked into town, he wouldn't have talked to me at all.

The woman passed me the envelope from the Ministry of Education. She gave me two letters as well. I thanked her and left.

"What are you doing now?" Owen asked. He was following me everywhere.

"I'm going to read my letters."

I opened the first one.

Dear Nicky,

I just wanted to write and tell you that you are my best friend ever. I enjoy playing chess with you, even though you always beat me. I like it when you beat me! You always help me with my homework. Thanks!

Love,

Your best friend for life

The second one read:

Dear Nicky,

I heard that you scored 125% on your last spelling test. Wow! That means you actually spelled more words than they asked for. That's amazing! I'm proud to be your friend.

Love,

Your second best friend for life

"Wanna do something?" Owen asked.

I folded up the letters and put them in my pocket. "I have to go to the store," I said. Mom had reminded me as I was leaving the camper. "Nicky! We're out of rollmops!"

"I'll go with you," said Owen. "Hey! Do you want to sign my cast?"

I hadn't noticed the cast on his arm until he rolled up his sleeve. I could see lots of names written on it — Mary, Ingrid, Joe, Alice, Dylan, Ms Went. Someone with that many friends had to be genuinely nice. Besides, no one had ever asked me to sign his cast before.

"Do you have a pen?" I asked.

"We can borrow one at the store."

Owen showed me where the store was, though I could easily have found it on my own. Encore was tiny, yet they still had rollmops at the Co-op. I'd hoped they wouldn't, but I was wrong. I bought four jars and Owen didn't say anything about them. He asked the cashier for a pen and I signed his cast Nicky H.H. Grant. He didn't ask about the H.H. either, so I started to like him. Then he said something that almost made me cry with happiness.

"Wanna come to my house?"

The kids I met on the road always wanted to see where the circus people lived. They never imagined I might want to see an ordinary house.

"I have to bring the groceries back," I said. "We can go to your place after that."

"Okay," said Owen, and we rode away friends.

"Maybe you can have supper with us," he said a minute later.

"Really?"

"Sure. I'll ask my mom."

I wondered what they would be having for supper. Carrots, I hoped. Or green beans. Maybe after supper we could do our homework together!

"Can you skid on that thing?" he asked.

"No."

"Watch this." He pedalled crazily up the road then slammed on the brakes. We got down and measured his skid mark in the dust. It was almost two metres long!

"Can I try the unicycle?" Owen asked.

"Sure."

"You can try my bike."

"That's all right," I said.

I have a confession to make. Please don't blab it around. I actually don't know how to ride a bicycle. There. Now you know. I was too embarrassed to admit it to Owen. How do you do it on two wheels instead of just one? It's got to be twice as hard.

The big top was set up just outside town in a farmer's field, with the campers in a circle behind it. No one was around when we arrived. They were having a meeting with Mr. Fudge to discuss the show that night. Owen couldn't believe his eyes when he saw our camper. "Where did you get all this stuff?" He meant the things glued all over it.

"Pink Pelican Popcorn mostly," I told him. "I'm just going to leave my parents a note so they know where I am." I took the rollmops and my mail inside.

"I have some plastic astronauts," Owen said when I came out. "If I gave them to you, would you stick them on?"

"Sure. Let's go."

First he wanted to try the unicycle. He managed to get up on the seat by gripping the side of the camper. Very carefully, he wheeled forward using the gewgaws as handholds.

I walked beside him. "Do you have your own room?"

"Yeah."

"Really?"

"Sure. Who doesn't?"

I didn't volunteer an answer. "Is there a bathtub at your house?"

He laughed. "Of course."

When he'd made it completely around the camper, I asked if we could go. "Your house sounds wonderful," I said.

Then I heard crying (my brother, of course) and, a moment later, laughter: my dad's great guffaws and my mom's shrieks. The Fantastic Flyers were leaving Mr. Fudge's camper and heading to their own campers for an early supper before the show. Owen stared as the acrobats, Mimi and Claude, cartwheeled along. Bruce the Strongish Man gave Grandma Jack a helpful shove through her door. "Time to re-grease the door frame!" she called out. Coco yapped around everyone's heels and sprang into the air and did a back flip.

"Who have we here?" Mom and Dad cried when they saw Owen. "A friend! A friend for Nicky! He's always wanted a friend!"

"I'm going to his house for supper," I announced.

"Oh, eat here, son! We want to get to know —
what's your name?" they asked.

"Owen."

"Owen!" Dad put out his hand.

"Don't!" I cried.

Owen did.

BUZZZ! He fell off the unicycle.

Dad picked him up and threw him in the air.
Luckily, he caught him coming down. Sometimes
Dad would get distracted and let Saggy hit the
ground.

Right now Saggy was crying that his tummy
hurt. Mom carried him inside the camper. Dad
carried Owen. "We're eating at Owen's," I said
again.

Dad dropped Owen on the table and put his
hands behind his back. "Pick a hand, Owen, any
hand."

Owen picked one. Dad gave him two tickets to
the circus. "How many people in your family,
Owen?"

"Three," said Owen.

Dad handed him the two tickets that were in
his other hand. "Bring a friend," he said.

I'm his friend! I wanted to say. But I didn't want

to go to the circus. I'd seen it six hundred and thirteen times.

Mom started making dinner on the little stove, with Saggy clinging like a monkey to her back. The louder he cried, the louder she laughed. "Inside-out burgers!" she called.

"What are inside-out burgers?" Owen asked me.

"They're not very good," I said. "We'd better eat at your house." But Dad was setting out supper.

When Owen saw the bowl of marshmallows and the boxes of Pink Pelican Popcorn, he took a seat.

"Good. You're staying," Dad said, juggling the plates. "But I should warn you, Owen. We don't eat vegetables here."

Owen grinned. "Fine by me!"

Inside-out burgers, in case you don't know, are two meat patties with a bun in the middle. We have them on Thursday nights, with marshmallows and Pink Pelican Popcorn for dessert. After supper we go out with the crazy glue and stick the prizes to the camper.

"You seem like a happy-go-lucky sort of kid, Owen," Dad said during the meal. "Look at Nicky here. A Very Serious Child. And his brother Saggy. Always in the dumps over something."

"He gets a lot of tummy aches," Mom explained with a laugh.

"We love them to bits, of course. But they're definitely not circus material."

"Maybe Nicky isn't really our son," Mom said.

"Ha ha," I said.

"He's your son, for sure," Dad told Mom. "He's got your nose."

Mom patted her face. "Nicky! Have you got my nose? Give it back right now! I need it for tonight."

I wanted to crawl under the table, but Owen laughed and laughed.

"Oh my galoshes!" Mom shrieked. "Look at the time!"

We all hurried out to glue our prizes on the camper. I had a miniature harmonica and Owen a pair of dice. Saggy got a rubber snake, Mom some plastic teeth and Dad a diamond ring. Then Mom and Dad had to start putting on their make-up.

"Are you coming to the show, Owen?" Dad asked.

Of course Owen was coming. He had free tickets. He got on his bike and rode home to tell his mom and dad. "I'll see you there, Nicky!" he called.

But I didn't go to the show that night. I stayed in the camper with Saggy instead.

"Are you sad, Nicky?" my little brother asked.

"I'm okay," I said.

It's hard having funny parents. They always steal the show, even when the show's not on. As for Owen, we were moving on in a few days anyway, and I would never see him again. He was just another true friend I never made.

At least I had Split A Gut. We curled up in our cozy bunk. I read him the hard words out of the dictionary and, together, we marvelled at their meanings.

Rollmops

Fun. That was what Mom and Dad lived for. And to make people laugh. I'm not saying they were bad parents. Saggy and I love them a lot. Maybe you feel the same way about your parents. Maybe you love them but still wish they were completely different people sometimes.

Because our parents lived for fun, we were only allowed to eat funny food. You probably have rules about food at your house. Probably your mom and dad won't let you have candy until you've eaten a proper dinner. I bet you have milk at mealtimes because pop is a special treat. For us, it was the opposite. We had pop at mealtimes and milk was the treat. Our diet was mostly marshmallows, popcorn, candy, cookies, hamburgers (inside-out), French fries, hot dogs and pizza. The pizza was pepperoni, with the pepperoni slices arranged in a clown face.

Those are your favourite foods, aren't they? "What's that Nicky H.H. Grant complaining about?" you're probably saying to yourself. But think. Would they still be your favourite  foods if you had to eat them *every single day of your life*?

We were only allowed cereal that was coloured and came in funny shapes — rings or hearts or four-leaf clovers — and only if there was a prize at the bottom of the box or a contest you could enter. We could never eat cereal at breakfast either. No! That wouldn't be any fun! Friday nights were cereal nights. For breakfast, we had rollmops.

Do you know what a rollmop is? No? Why you lucky, lucky kid! When you go to bed tonight and lie there thinking about all the good things in your life, add to your list the fact that you've never tasted, or maybe even heard of, a rollmop.

The smell is hideous. As soon as Mom opened

the jar in the morning, the little camper would fill with a fishy fog. Saggy and I would gag and rush to a window for fresh air while Mom and Dad stuck their noses in the jar. Then Mom would divide up the horrible contents between us. "What a perfect food," she always said, because you don't need a serving spoon or plates or knives and forks to eat a rollmop. Rollmops come stabbed through with toothpicks. She'd pluck one out and hand it to Saggy. Saggy would start to cry. "Eat it," she'd say. "Eat it! It will make you grow up to be a clown."

When I was young I believed this. I choked down my rollmops and waited for the funny feeling to come. It never did, so when I got older I began to have doubts. One day I went to see Mr. Fudge because I knew he'd give me a straight answer.

He opened his door and, bowing, ushered me inside. "Have a seat, Nicky."

His rabbit, Sir John A., was sitting on it. "Sir John," Mr. Fudge said to the rabbit. "I'm asking you respectfully. We have a guest."

The rabbit pulled an ear forward and washed behind it with his paw. Sighing, Mr. Fudge put on his top hat and began poking around the camper for his wand. If Sir John had been your rabbit, you would probably have just picked him off the chair, right? Me too, but circus people use every opportunity to keep their skills up.

While Mr. Fudge searched I looked at the pictures on his wall — at the bear in the tutu, at Mr. Fudge's head sticking out of a soft mountain of white rabbits (distant cousins of Sir John A.) and at Carlo the Great, who had taught Mr. Fudge every trick he knew. The picture of glaring and smiling Sal-Sally was in its special place on the bedside table, with a red plastic rose tucked into its frame.

"Ah! There it is."

Mr. Fudge's wand was with his toothbrush, in a glass by the sink. He flicked it at the chair and Sir John A. disappeared, but I felt the seat before I sat down on it anyway, just in case. "Now," said Mr. Fudge, taking the chair across from me. "What can I do for you, Nicky?"

"I have a question. I'd like an honest answer."

"This sounds serious. Do you mind if I smoke?"

"Don't smoke, Mr. Fudge. It's bad for you."

"You're wise beyond your years, son," he said, taking a cigar out of his breast pocket. "No need to worry, though. It's tobacco-free." He sniffed the whole length of the cigar to make sure my dad hadn't switched it as a joke. He chuckled. "Your father's cigars are the worst kind for you, Nicky. They explode."

He bit the end off and, extending a hand, asked me to pull a finger.

"No."

"Go on."

"No," I said.

"Don't worry. I'm no Mr. Toots. Pull it."

I pulled one of his fingers. As soon as I let go, the tip burst into flame. I could hardly believe my eyes! He lit the cigar with it and coughed.

"Mr. Fudge. I've never seen that trick before."

"I've been practising it for forty years now. Usually something else starts on fire. I guess I finally got it right." He blew the flaming finger out. "Okay. What's your question?"

"Is it true . . ." I began.

"Sir John!" Mr. Fudge roared. "This is the limit!" He snatched the top hat off his head. Brown pellets hailed onto the table. "How embarrassing," he muttered as he brushed his shoulders clean. "All right. Your question. I won't interrupt any more, I promise."

He looked very seriously across the table at me, with Sir John A. sitting on his head.

"Is it true, Mr. Fudge, that if you eat rollmops for breakfast you'll grow up to be a clown?"

He sucked thoughtfully on the cigar. Sir John A.'s nose twitched. "There's more than one way to grow up to be a clown, Nicky," he finally said, and puffs of smoke trailed his words. "That's certainly one of them. A rollmop for breakfast every morning and you're guaranteed a sense of humour for life."

"I don't want to grow up to be a clown," I said.

Mr. Fudge blinked. "You don't?"

"No."

"What do you want to be, then?"

"An accountant," I told him.

Tears filled his eyes, though it might have been because the camper was so smoky. "An accountant. That's something greatly needed in a circus that no one ever thinks of. Good boy, Nicky." He reached out and patted my head.

Later I found a quarter stuck to my hair. I had to cut it off with scissors.

Back to the rollmops.

I'd plug my nose as Mom passed me my serving. Then I'd close my eyes, because I didn't want to see it actually going in. I'd learned that it was less horrible if I slid it off the toothpick in one mouthful, and chewed as little as possible so less of the taste escaped. Poor Saggy. His mouth was too small. He had to take two or three bites. He'd bawl his head off until he managed to swallow it all. Of course, Coco loved rollmops. She even wanted to eat the toothpick, but we wouldn't let her.

Though I tried not to look at my morning rollmop, I'll describe it to you, so you'll understand. It's a fish! A shiny silver fish still wearing its skin. At least the head gets chopped off in the Rollmop

Processing Plant. The fish is wrapped around a chunk of pickle and stuck through with a toothpick so it doesn't come free and start swimming around in the jar. That's the "roll" part, I guess. The pickle must be the "mop."

Don't go looking for them in the grocery store because they're sure to be there.

They're always there.

Size 44

The reason Mr. Fudge was so choked up when I said I wanted to be an accountant, besides the smoke, of course, is that the circus always had money troubles. There never seemed to be enough to keep the tent and equipment in repair or to pay the performers on time. Worse, when Mr. Fudge finally made his overdue rounds to pay everyone, they would run off and spend it all right away. They didn't know how to budget. The situation was hardest for my parents, who had me and Saggy to feed and clothe and school. Not that they took those responsibilities very seriously. They weren't serious about anything. Lucky for us, the circus was like one big family. Everyone pitched in to raise us kids.

As I said, Mr. Fudge arranged my schooling. Saggy was still too young. Grandma Jack was the one who clothed us because she would head to

the thrift store whenever there was one in town. Grandma Jack shopped in thrift stores because she had to wear two size 22 dresses at the same time. One dress wasn't big enough. She'd snip out a side seam on each dress and remove the sleeve, then sew the two dresses together to make a size 44.

22 + 22 = 44

Sometimes Mimi helped Grandma Jack. Mimi and her husband, Claude, our acrobats last year, were French, from Montreal. Mimi liked to advise Grandma Jack on what she should add to each dress to make it *haute couture*, which is French for "high sewing." She'd draw a little sketch on the back of a popcorn bag and Grandma Jack would sew on all the feathers and beads and frills. When she saw herself in the latest creation, she'd laugh and say, "It may be high, but it's just as *wide!*"

It's hard on a body to be that big. That's what Grandma Jack said when her back gave her trouble last June. She was helping to raise the big top in Halo, Saskatchewan. We all heard a loud *CRACK* and thought lightning had struck the pole. "There she goes," said Grandma. The only thing for it was flat-out bedrest.

Grandma Jack's heart was under a lot of strain as well. It could "go" too, at any time. Everybody agreed it had been a mistake to let her help with the heavy work. The problem was she hated to feel useless. Now she kept wailing from her bed, "Who's going to sell the tickets?"

Mom and Dad asked me to make sure Grandma Jack didn't get too fidgety while she was recovering, so I went to town to buy her a paper. I got the community news, which was mostly farm reports and town gossip. I was afraid the city paper would get her worked up, since it was sure to be filled with horrible happenings in the world that she would be helpless to do anything about.

As I was paying, the storekeeper said, "You're with the circus, eh? Make sure Mr. Timchuk gets a free ticket."

I guessed that Mr. Timchuk was the farmer whose field we were using. We always gave free tickets in exchange for hospitality. I told this to the storekeeper.

"That's good because Timchuk could use a laugh. He's had nothing but bad luck. Last year his spleen went. Then he gets hit with the drought like everyone else. He decides to get out of grain altogether, go into chickens. Now his incubator's kaput."

You know. The machine that keeps the eggs warm until they hatch.

There was a display of wooden Ukrainian Easter eggs next to the cash register. I bought one as a souvenir to glue on the camper. On the way back, I picked Grandma Jack some wildflowers.

"Aren't you a dear, Nicky," she said. "Put them in water. Thank you. Set them there. Yes, where I can see them."

"I brought you the paper too."

"Nicky! You're my best boy. Can you sit and visit with me a minute?"

I sat and fanned her with the newspaper and showed her the painted wooden egg. Then I asked, "Where's your spleen, Grandma Jack?"

"Somewhere in here," she said, shaking her belly. "Where's yours?"

"Same place, I guess. What's it for?"

"Same as tonsils. And your appendix. Good for nothing, just like Grandma Jack when her back's hurt and she's got to lie here like a beached whale! Who's gonna sell the popcorn?"

I told her why I was asking — because of the farmer's troubles. His spleen, the weather, the broken incubator, I told her the whole story.

"The poor man," Grandma Jack tsk-tsked. "Some people get more than their share of bad luck."

After a while I left her with the newspaper so I could go glue the egg on our camper. "Nicky! Nicky!" I heard her calling before I'd finished the job. I went running.

"It says here that the company that made that incubator can't get the part to Mr. Timchuk until the week after next! By then the chicks will be dead! Hundreds of them!"

I stared at her, afraid. She was all steamed up and waving the paper in the air. Her heart could go! And where exactly? Where Mr. Timchuk's spleen went? Where her back went? Can parts of

your body just disappear like a white rabbit?

"Please calm down, Grandma Jack," I begged.

"I feel so useless!" she moaned.

I asked for the paper back, in case there was more bad news in it. I said I wanted to make a hat out of it for Saggy. Before she handed it over, she pointed to the headline:

Chickens doomed, farmer says

"A tragedy," Grandma Jack said.

Grandma Jack was soft. Soft-hearted and soft-bodied. All my life she had looked after me while my mom and dad performed. I remembered nestling under the wide flap of her arm, as warm and safe as under a mother bird's wing. I remembered that feeling. Then I got an idea.

"Grandma Jack?" I said. "I think we can save those chicks."

She sent me to speak to Mr. Timchuk. I took Saggy and together we trudged across his dusty field. Above it the sky was a bright blue big top stretched over the whole province, not a cloud in sight.

At the farmhouse, a man came to the door with the saddest face I'd ever seen. "Yes?" he said.

"We're with Mr. Fudge's Fantastic Flyers," I explained. "We heard about your bad luck and think we can help."

He shook his head. "It'll take ten days for that new part to get here. Those chicks won't last through another cold night."

"Come and see Grandma Jack," Saggy said.

"She'd be happy to keep those eggs warm," I explained.

Mr. Timchuk came with us. I could tell he didn't believe the plan would work until he laid eyes on Grandma Jack in her big bed and saw for himself all her warm folds of flesh. "You can tuck them in all over me," she said. "I've got seven chins where a dozen eggs should fit."

"We can try," he said. "But what if you roll over?"

"I can't budge," Grandma Jack assured him. "My back's gone."

Saggy and I got our pillows from our camper, then went with Mr. Timchuk to load the eggs into his truck. We carried the trays on the pillows, in case we dropped them. Then we rode in the truck back to Grandma Jack's camper. We let Mr. Timchuk tuck in the eggs. By then everyone knew what was happening and had gathered to watch the delicate operation through the camper windows. Once all the eggs were nestled around and among Grandma Jack, Mr. Timchuk declared that nobody would believe what we'd done. That was when I came up with my other idea.

"What would you think, Grandma Jack, about selling tickets?"

We had to take the roof off Grandma Jack's camper, but we'd done that before, the time she got stuck inside. Bruce the Strongish Man lifted out the bed, with a little help.

"Careful!" Grandma Jack cried. "Don't drop me or they'll break!"

We put up the smaller tent around the bed and charged a dollar to get in. After Mr. Fudge phoned the paper to announce the special sideshow event, people came from all around, particularly the farmers who are always interested in new agricultural techniques. Farmers are very patient people. This must come from having to depend on the weather for your livelihood. They'd been waiting months for rain. Now they sat on chairs and waited days for those eggs to hatch. Soon there were so many people we put Grandma Jack under the big top during the day, when the show wasn't on. We sold landslides of popcorn, cloud banks of candy floss.

Mr. Fudge took me aside. "Nicky, do you realize that the Fantastic Flyers could have gone broke by the end of the summer if we hadn't added this attraction? I want to thank you."

I said, "Don't thank me. Thank size 44."

"A tickle behind my left ear," Grandma Jack announced on the fifth day. "I think some little chick is trying to stretch his wings."

When word got around that the hatching had finally begun, the stands packed with cheering spectators. Grandma Jack laughed and laughed as each yellow puff popped out of its shell. "Just like popcorn! Oh, stop! Stop! It tickles!"

Soon the warm mountain of Grandma Jack swarmed with chicks. When Bruce took her arms and hauled her to a seated position, the chicks scattered, but they hurried back. They wouldn't stray from her cozy body for long. Grandma Jack was their mother now.

Grandma Jack raised her arms to hush the crowd. She bowed slowly forward, then straightened, testing out her back. "It's all right," she declared. "I feel fine now. All I needed was a lie-down."

Jail Birds

Last night I read to Saggy what I've written so far. He liked the last chapter best, but thought the chapter about Owen was too sad. "And why am I always crying?" he asked.

"Because you were always crying," I said.

"Why?"

"Because your tummy hurt. Don't you remember?"

"No," Saggy said. "And you didn't tell about when Mom and Dad got thrown in jail."

"I'm getting to that."

After Grandma Jack hatched the chicks, we had to stay on in Halo for another week. The chicks weren't ready to leave Grandma Jack. They followed her wherever she went like a fluffy yellow train attached to her size 44 dress. Mimi oo-*la*-*la*-ed every time the procession went past. "That is

the most *jolie* robe I have ever see!" Which means she thought it was *haute couture*. The chicks still needed to sleep with Grandma's warmth at night. When Mr. Timchuk's incubator part arrived, he took them back, and we moved on according to our schedule.

My parents' eleventh anniversary came around during that time and they decided to go out to dinner to celebrate. Because Mom spent almost half her life as Ms Toots, she always found her real face in the mirror a little colourless. "Is my lipstick all right?" she asked as she was getting ready.

"It's red. Is it supposed to be?" Dad answered.

"I like these cheerful pop cans," she said. She always used pop cans as rollers because they gave her the big curl she liked. "I think I'll wear them out to dinner. What do you think, Len?"

Dad said, "You always look funny to me, Red."

When they were ready to go, they kissed us goodbye. "We hope you boys will get into trouble while we're gone."

Saggy started to cry.

For the record, we've never gotten into trouble. We've never broken a dish or spilled a drink or forgotten to flush the toilet and wash our hands. We've never had a temper tantrum or sassed our parents or read under the covers after the light has been turned out. We've never searched their pockets for change to spend. There wouldn't be any. Swear words? We don't know any.

"You can't take Coco," I said.

"What?" they said.

"Dogs aren't allowed in restaurants."

"They aren't?" said Mom and Dad. "Why not?"

"It's not hygienic." (For your information, hygienic means clean.)

"Coco's hygienic!" they cried.

"What's hygienic?" Dad asked.

"I don't know, but it's outrageous for you to suggest she's not!" Mom shouted at Dad.

"I never suggested such a thing!" he yelled back.

"Liar!"

They started to throw punches, but soft ones. They were only pretending to argue.

In the end, we shut Coco in the camper with us. She yapped and tried to scratch through the door. "Have a wonderful time," I said, presenting them with two boxes of Pink Pelican Popcorn wrapped in newspaper. Saggy stopped crying soon after they left, but he started again later, when they'd been gone a while.

"It hasn't been *that* long," I told him. We often stayed in the camper while Mom and Dad performed. Grandma Jack would look in on us from time to time. Saggy was just nervous because he knew they weren't close by in the big top tonight.

I tried to teach him how to play chess, but he couldn't remember how the pieces moved. He kept wanting the knights to have a horse race. Then several hours did pass without Mom and Dad returning. Where could they be? I put Saggy to bed and read him a few pages of the dictionary until he fell asleep. Careful to keep Coco in, I slipped out to ask Mr. Fudge's advice.

When I knocked, there was no answer. A light was on, so I peeked in Mr. Fudge's window and saw him slumped in his chair, hugging the picture of Sal-Sally. Sir John A. was on his lap, licking the tears off his face.

"Sal-Sally? Sal-Sally? Why do you make me wait?"

Poor Mr. Fudge. He only wanted the happiness my parents had.

There was nothing to do then but go and let Coco out.

Twenty minutes later she came back, barking crazily. "*Shh*," I said. "You'll wake everyone up." I wrote a note and taped it to the camper door:

Gone rescuing

You should never leave the house without letting an adult know where you're going. And if you have a little brother who can't read yet, you should draw him a picture. I drew myself taking Coco for a walk and left it on the table in case Saggy woke up.

Coco ran ahead. I knew Mom and Dad were in serious trouble by the way Coco was barking and how she kept circling behind me and nipping at my heels, trying to hurry me along. When we reached the main street of town, Coco ran off.

You already know where they were, because Saggy told you. You're not one bit surprised. But I was, let me tell you, when I realized Coco was bringing me to the police station. She ran up the stone steps and yipped to get in. Until then, I'd been worried about them. Now I was afraid. Mom and Dad are innocent and trusting, like children. I felt responsible for them. If something bad had happened, I'd never forgive myself.

Coco tugged my pant leg. When I opened the door, she scooted in.

"Hey! No dogs allowed!"

A very grumpy-looking police officer got up from his desk. We had to chase Coco around the room for several minutes before we managed to catch her, but not before she bit the officer. "Hey!" he bellowed at me. "I could fine you for this!"

The officer tossed Coco outside, then disappeared down a hall. I could hear what sounded like a party going on behind a door with a little barred window — laughter and cheering that Coco's barking had drowned out. The officer came back with a bandage around the finger Coco had tasted. "What do you want?" he said.

"I think my parents are here."

"Those clowns? Ho ho! Get them out of here."

"I'll take them now," I said.

"Did you bring bail?"

"How much is the bail?" I asked.

"Five hundred."

"Dollars?" I asked.

"I'm not talking kicks in the pants."

"I don't have five hundred dollars."

"Tough luck," he said.

I was quite surprised by his tone of voice, having always understood that the police are there to help. I hope after reading this you'll still go the police if you're in trouble. Chances are you won't get this guy. Remember, too, that Coco had just bitten him, which might account for his bad mood.

A great roar came from behind the door, followed by hooting and clapping. Then the door swung open and a second officer appeared. He was chuckling to himself, but he put on a serious look as soon as he saw the first officer's scowl.

"Hello," he said to me, kindly. "Who are you?"

"Clowns' kid," the grumpy officer said. "He can't post bail."

"Don't worry, son," said the nice officer. "The

judge will see them in a day or two. Until then, we'll keep good care of them." His face crumpled and he started to laugh again.

I wanted to cry. They wouldn't have rollmops at the police station! Also, there was a performance the next night.

"The show can't go on without Mr. and Ms Toots!"

The nice officer buckled right over, holding his belly. Officer Grumpy snatched up the phone in disgust.

"Who are you calling?" the nice officer managed to ask.

"The Pink Pearl."

"Getting takeout?"

From the half of the conversation I could hear, I figured out that Grumpy was talking to the owners of the restaurant where my parents had eaten that night. I pieced together what had happened. They'd forgotten to bring any money! When Grumpy hung up, he said, "Settle their bill and they can go."

"How much is it?" I asked.

"Thirteen seventy. That's dollars."

"I'll be right back," I said.

"Better include a tip!" Grumpy shouted after me.

I ran back with Coco and, quietly, so I wouldn't wake Saggy, got twenty dollars out of the rollmop jar above the stove. Coco wasn't happy when I shut her in the camper again, but I couldn't take her with me. If she bit Grumpy a second time, I'd end up in jail myself. If she barked, she'd wake Saggy, so I was forced to plug a striped sock in her mouth. I ran all the way back to town.

"This money smells like fish," Grumpy told me when I handed it to him, breathless. He took it anyway and Officer Nice went and got Mom and Dad.

"Nicky!" they cried when they saw me. "How lovely of you to come!"

Dad tried to shake the officers' hands. "Oh, no," Grumpy said. "I'm not going to fall for that again." Mom, the pop cans still in her hair, kissed Officer Nice. As we left the station, she said, "I do believe that was the most fun we've ever had on our anniversary."

"But you went to jail!" I said.

"The people were so friendly."

"What people?" I asked.

"The people in jail with us."

"They were criminals," I reminded them.

"Yes, but they hadn't done anything serious."

We reached the outskirts of town where the huge prairie night hung above us, winking with stars. "That one officer did seem in a funk," Dad admitted.

"So were the people in the restaurant," Mom said. "You won't believe it, Nicky. They preferred to be paid in money. Apparently jokes are not acceptable."

"They were such funny jokes too," Dad said, shaking his head.

"Mr. Hope split a gut."

"Who's Mr. Hope?" I asked.

"A very nice vagrant we met tonight. And that drunk man who couldn't remember his name? What a great sense of humour."

"We should have brought you and Saggy," Dad said.

I didn't say anything.

Mom kissed me. "Next year," she said. "I promise."

The Lees

There was something funny going on. Well, there was always something funny going on, but this was funny peculiar, funny mysterious, not funny ha ha. No matter how many gewgaws we glued on the camper, there was always space. How could that be? The camper glittered with popcorn booty and the souvenirs of dying towns. On sunny days (every day was sunny), you had to shield your eyes to look at it. But every Thursday night we'd run out with more prizes and always find places to glue them on.

"Maybe it's a magic camper," Saggy suggested.

"Maybe some prizes are falling off," Dad said.

But we'd been in Halo for close to two weeks, the longest we'd ever stayed in any one place during the touring season, waiting for Mr. Timchuk's incubator part. We walked all around the camper. No prizes had fallen on the ground. Saggy crawled under it. No prizes.

"Someone's stealing them," I said.

"No!" Mom and Dad gasped. They refused to believe we had a thief in our midst.

"I'll hide," I said. "I'll catch them."

"We'll hide too," they said. "Nobody will come."

We crawled under the camper, joining Saggy, and Coco too, because she never wanted to be left out. For over an hour we lay in wait, cramped in the dust. Saggy fell asleep. I grew thirsty and wished seriously I wasn't such a serious and suspicious child. Just as I was about to give up, feet approached the camper. Lots of feet. Four big feet and six small feet, all wearing the same shoes, flat-soled and made of red cloth with a single strap and buckle.

"I know those shoes," Mom whispered. "Where do I know them from?"

"Where?" Dad asked.

"I'm asking you."

"How should I know?"

"I'm just asking."

"Shh!" I said, not wanting to give our hiding place away. We waited to see if the people in these shoes would pry prizes off the camper. They didn't. They spoke to each other in a language we couldn't understand, then knocked loudly on the camper door.

"The Pink Pearl," Mom whispered.

"Is that a kind of popcorn?" Dad asked.

"The restaurant! These are the owners of the restaurant!" Mom hissed. "Hide!"

"We're hiding already," I said.

"Nicky, you are the smartest boy."

The night before, I'd rescued them from the police station. Now the owners of the restaurant had come to see us. We had no idea why, but it couldn't be for a reason favourable to us.

Then a head, upside down, appeared before us wearing an upside-down smile. "Hello. I am Mr.

Lee. Remember?" He pointed to his nose. "Mr. Lee. Pink Pearl restaurant."

"How do you do, Mr. Lee?" Dad said, and he stuck his hand out from under the camper.

BUZZZ!

The startled, upside-down Mr. Lee shook out his hand. "How are you today?" he asked.

"Very well, thank you. We certainly enjoyed the meal last night. Fortune cookies are among my favourite foods."

"Every fortune I got was fortunate!" Mom said.

Mr. Lee wore a blank expression. His face disappeared momentarily while more Chinese was spoken.

When he looked back under the camper, Dad introduced us. "Mr. Lee? These are our children, Saggy and Nicky. You didn't meet them last night."

Mr. Lee nodded to us. "Please," he said. "Please come out."

We decided that they weren't going to give us any trouble. The Lees must have decided the same thing about Mom and Dad before they came. So we crawled out and brushed ourselves off, but we were all going to need a sponge bath that night.

The Lee family stood before us, dressed identically in yellow track suits and red shoes. There was a mother and father and two teenage daughters and a boy who looked about seven but who, I soon found out, was my own age then, nine. The mother and the girls had their hair done in the same style, two tight buns on either side, like bears' ears. They held sticks with long red ribbons attached to one end. The boy had a tooth-filled smile except for a gap in front and, strangely, a small bald patch on the top of his head.

It was the boy, Gim, who took over the talking from there.

"Have you heard of the Shanghai Circus?"

"Why, it's world-famous!" Mom and Dad exclaimed.

You can probably guess their story. The year before, the Lees had come to Canada on a tour and decided not to go back to China with the other members of their troupe. Apparently China is very crowded. They liked the wide open spaces of the Canadian prairie and the fact that there's a Chinese restaurant in every little town. In some towns you can actually buy a house for a dollar. They bought one in Halo, which left them with enough money to buy the Pink Pearl too. But they didn't realize how much they would miss performing.

"Nicky," Mom said. "Go get Mr. Fudge."

He was shaving in his camper, but on hearing the name Shanghai Circus he dropped the razor and came with me, half of his face still coated with lather. He looked only half like Mr. Fudge.

The Lee family performed one of their routines right there in the circle of the campers. They leaped and tumbled, then rose up together in the shapes of pyramids and stars and flowers.

Then Mr. Lee stood with his arms in the air supporting Mrs. Lee, who did a handstand on his hands. One daughter stood on the soles of Mrs. Lee's feet and held up her sister the same way. Gim balanced at the very top. All at once they collapsed into a ball and rolled across the grass. The girls broke free and performed amazing tricks with the ribboned sticks. We were astounded, even more so when Mr. Lee magically produced boards and bricks, which he broke effortlessly over little Gim's bare head. We roared and cheered, and tears of joy washed the lather off Mr. Fudge's half-shaved face.

"Saved," he cried. "Saved again."

The next day the chicks went back to Mr. Timchuk's farm. We folded down the tents and broke camp and moved on to the next town. The Lees hung a sign on the door of their restaurant:

CLOSED

UNTIL FURTHER NOTICE

A School Day

"Have you ever been to school?" I asked Gim. It was our second day in the new town and we were sprawled in the grass playing Go, a Chinese game that's as exciting as chess. The board is a grid and you take turns filling it with black and white stones. Gim always beat me, though I was improving.

"I went to school all last year," he told me. "I was going to school last week. Then your mom and dad showed up at the restaurant."

I hung my head. "Sorry." But secretly I was glad, because now I had a friend. "Mr. Fudge will register you for a correspondence course," I said. "We can do our homework together."

Gim scratched at his bald patch, which itched him a lot. He laid down his white stone. "Let's just go to school."

"What?"

"There's a school here in Whynot. Let's just go. Tomorrow."

I looked at him seriously. Why not?

Remember your first day of school ever? Remember how excited and nervous you were? Remember wondering if the teacher would be nice and the kids friendly and if you would understand the rules? But imagine you aren't five or six, but *nine and a half*.

I could barely sleep that night.

Circus people sleep in every day because they work late. I had no trouble waking up earlier than everyone else. The night before, I'd set out my best clothes and dug the dirt out of the soles of my runners with a stick. Now I ate my rollmops and brushed my teeth three times to make sure my breath didn't smell like fish. I fixed my hair with a wet comb. Then I packed the best lunch I could with what we had and went out to meet Gim in the farmer's field.

Of course I left a note.

"What grade do you want to be in?" Gim asked as we walked.

"Can we choose?"

"Today we can. They'll just move us if we're not in the right class. When I started school they put me in Grade One even though I was eight."

"Why?"

"I couldn't speak English."

"Really? You speak it perfectly now."

"At Christmas they jumped me to Grade Three."

"Let's go to Grade Five today," I said. I figured if we were only staying in Whynot a few days, we might as well learn as much as we could.

It was easy to find the school because just as we got to town we spotted a yellow school bus turning a corner. We followed it and saw a low brick building at the end of the street. We heard the school too — happy screams and laughter, then the bell.

"Better run," I said.

The kids were still making their way to their classrooms when we arrived. I stopped a girl and asked her the way to Grade Five.

"That's Ms Went's class," she said, pointing.

All the kids were reading books when we came in. "Free reading time," Gim whispered. He went over to a shelf and grabbed a book for each of us. I was glad to have someone with me who knew the ropes.

I found a desk and started to read, but hadn't gotten very far when I heard, *"Psst."* I looked up. Across the aisle from me was a familiar face. It was Owen, my old un-friend, smiling and waving at me. He'd got his cast off.

Then the teacher started taking attendance. Ms Went looked about my mom's age, whatever that is. She had blond hair that flipped up and a sweater over her shoulders. Every time she called a name, a kid answered, "Here."

"Owen Locke?"

"Here," said Owen.

Gim's and my name weren't called so we didn't say anything.

We did math first and it was easy. I noticed the other kids put up their hands to answer a question.

I liked that and decided I'd do it with my corre-spondence work from now on. My hand went up without thinking. I mean, I was thinking of the answer, but not about the fact that I was a stranger in the class.

"Forty-four," I said.

Ms Went smiled. "Correct . . ." Then she looked at me a second time. "Who are you?"

All the kids laughed.

"That's Nicky," said Owen.

"Nicky H.H. Grant," I said.

"Nicky. Welcome. You're obviously new here. Class, say hi to Nicky."

"Hi, Nicky," everyone said.

It was a very friendly group, just as I'd hoped.

A few minutes later Gim put up his hand to answer a question, and the same thing happened. "I guess we have two new students," said Ms Went, and everyone laughed again.

After math we had a spelling test. I got 100% even though I hadn't had the chance to study the words ahead of time. By then I was glad we'd chosen Grade Five because Grade Four would probably have been a waste of time.

Next we did Social Studies. The class was working on Canadian geography, which was a subject I knew a lot about, having seen so much of it in my nine years.

"Who remembers what the hills at the base of a mountain are called?" asked Ms Went.

I put up my hand. "Foothills."

"Correct, Nicky," she said.

I glanced over at Owen and was shocked to see that he had a comic book tucked inside his textbook.

"How about an isolated hill with steep sides and a flat top?"

I put up my hand again. "That's a butte."

"Right you are, Nicky."

I loved putting up my hand!

Then Ms Went said, very kindly, "Nicky? Would you mind giving the other kids a chance?"

She asked another question. "A gulch or valley with steep sides? What would that be?"

I pssted the answer to Owen. He grinned. Up went his hand.

"A coulee!" he shouted.

"So you *are* paying attention," said Ms Went. "Very good, Owen."

At recess Owen came right up to me and gave me five. I introduced him to Gim and he introduced us to his classmates. I remembered some of their names from his cast. Then he invited us to play tetherball, but I found it a little too dangerous. Gim shimmied up the pole and balanced on one hand at the top, showing off. The whole class gathered around, and everyone wanted to be his friend after that. I didn't mind sharing him, because I would be the one he walked home with.

When we came back to the classroom after recess, I suddenly noticed how beautiful Ms Went was. Just being away from her for fifteen minutes made me realize it.

I know what you're thinking, so that's all I'll say about it.

At lunch, the kids swarmed around me when they saw I'd brought popcorn and a can of Kool Kola. I was able to exchange them for Owen's ham sandwich and Ingrid's carrot sticks. Then Dylan offered me his apple for my slice of cold, soggy, clown-face pizza. What a deal!

"Gim," I said, "I think this is the happiest day of my life."

I wish it could have lasted.

After lunch, there was a knock on the classroom door. Ms Went answered it, then called for Gim and me. Gim looked worried, so I started to worry too.

It was the principal in a ferocious-looking suit.

"Gim? Nicky? This is Mr. Schlepp," said the wonderful Ms Went. "He'd like you to go down to the office and get registered."

As we followed him down the hallway, Gim nudged me and made a running motion with two fingers. I shook my head. No. I was staying. Mr. Schlepp opened the door to his office and waved us in. "You're a couple of serious ones," he said.

For some reason Gim had taken his baseball cap from his desk before leaving the classroom. Ms Went had made him take it off earlier, explaining that hats were not to be worn in school, only outside. That was the school rule. Now Gim was wearing his hat in the principal's office! I motioned for him to take it off. He looked straight ahead.

"Cap off, son," said Mr. Schlepp.

Gim took off the cap.

Mr. Schlepp asked us our names and our parents' names. I didn't know what I was going to say when he asked for our addresses. But before that, he asked Gim how to spell his mother's name. There was a Q and an X in it so he asked Gim to write it down.

Gim leaned over the desk to write.

"What's wrong with your head?" asked the principal.

"Nothing," said Gim.

"It's not nothing. It could be contagious."

Contagious, in case you don't know, means you can catch it. Mr. Schlepp was worried that the other kids in the school would catch what Gim had on the top of his head. But it was just worn-off hair, and a callus, a patch of hardened skin. People usually get calluses on their hands and feet. Bruce the Strongish Man has them from  lifting weights. I knew that Gim had a callus on the top of his head because that was where his father broke the bricks and boards in half. You can't catch a callus.

"Hold on a minute," said Mr. Schlepp. "I'm going to get the nurse to have a look."

The second he was out of the room, Gim sprang across the desk, slid open the window behind it and leaped out. "Nicky!" he called from outside.

Carefully, I got up on Mr. Schlepp's chair and looked out the window at Gim.

"Jump," Gim called.

"I can't. It's too far down."

"Come on!"

"Why?" I asked.

"When they find out that my dad breaks things over my head, they'll take me away. They'll take you away too."

"Really?"

"Yeah."

I started to climb through the window but got scared and stopped halfway. "I can't!"

I heard an angry voice behind me. "Young man! What do you think you're doing?"

I fell out the window. It hurt like crazy when I hit the ground but I had no time to cry about it. We started running.

We were never expelled, by the way. We couldn't be. We hadn't finished registering.

Runaways

Gim was my best friend. Because of him, I was very happy that the Lees had joined the Fantastic Flyers, but there was an unfortunate consequence too. The Lee children were performers, like their parents, and this gave Mom and Dad an idea.

"Would you like to get shot out of the cannon?" they asked at dinner.

"No!" we screamed.

"It's so much fun!"

"Never!" we cried.

"How about swallowing swords?"

They wanted to put Saggy and me in the circus! Until then, it had never occurred to them. We were horrified, and Saggy went straight to bed with his worst stomach ache ever.

At least we wouldn't end up like Gim. Poor Gim! He was a human chopping block. Gim said it didn't hurt him to have bricks broken over his head, but he was embarrassed that he had no hair on top. He told me it had only just started to grow back when they joined the Fantastic Flyers.

"And I need to get a proper education," Gim had said. "I want to be a dentist when I grow up."

After dinner Mom showed me a big bolt of polka-dot fabric she'd bought in town that day.

"What's that for?" I asked.

"I'm going to sew costumes for you and Saggy. Mimi's going to help."

She unrolled the fabric and made me lie down on it. Then she traced around my body with a pen.

"You're going to look so cute," she said.

I decided to run away.

Are you thinking what I think you're thinking? That in the last chapter we ran away from school because we were afraid of being taken away from our parents and now, here I was, planning to run away from *them*? But imagine my fate if I stayed: bottle-feeding a chihuahua wrapped up as a baby while riding around on a unicycle and squirting water out of a plastic daisy at a hundred people laughing their heads off at me. Does that sound like fun to you?

I slipped out to find Gim before the show to tell him my plan. He said he was coming too. Then I realized that if I left without Saggy, he'd be riding around on the unicycle with baby Coco all by himself. I had to give him the choice.

"Without Mom and Dad?" he asked.

"I'd rather they came too, but they won't."

Saggy decided to come.

Early the next morning we packed a few things and snuck away, while the camper was still filled with the sound of Mom's sleep-laughter and Dad's snores. We left a note. Always leave a note so your parents know where you are.

Dear Mom and Dad,

We love you so much but we don't want to be in the circus. We want to go to school and live in one place and eat vegetables, so we are running away. Gim is coming with us. Please let his parents know because he might not remember to leave them a note. We love you and hope to see you again some day.

Love,
Nicky and Saggy

Saggy started to cry so I looked around for a striped sock for his mouth.

Gim met us in the farmer's field. "We can't just run away to this town," he said. "We have to go at least to the next town, or they'll find us right away."

Saggy and I thought this was a good idea. We walked across the field to the highway without going into Whynot, in case people saw us.

It was a hot, dusty day. Several cars stopped and offered to give us a lift, but I knew it wasn't a good idea to get into a car with strangers, even though I was already tired of walking. We were all tired. Saggy was too tired even to cry so he put his hand in the striped sock and let it cry for a while.

"*Wa wa wa*," cried the sock.

We sat down in the ditch for a rest. Gim had brought food! He took a cardboard container of noodles out of his backpack. We'd

never tasted noodles before. They were delicious. Gim sucked each noodle through the space where a tooth was missing, claiming it tasted better that way. When I tried sucking, the noodle slapped me in the face.

We felt better after we'd eaten. Gim took Saggy on his back. He was strong, from being an acrobat. The striped sock napped.

When we finally reached the next town we

decided to stop there. The name was written on the grain elevator — Sonnet — and I remembered seeing it on the map and then looking it up in the dictionary. A sonnet is a fourteen-line rhyming poem. In Sonnet there's a post office, a store, a Chinese restaurant, some offices and five or six streets of small houses. There didn't seem to be a school. We'd have to take the bus.

"What now?" I asked.

Gim said, "Let's choose a house to live in."

"People are already living in these houses," I pointed out.

"We'll live with them," he said.

We walked up and down the streets, stopping at houses that looked promising. Not the ones that already had kids. If there were a lot of toys in the yard or kids' laundry on the clothesline, we walked right past. Also if there was a big, snarling dog. After we had walked up and down every street, we went to the Chinese restaurant and sat in a booth at the back. Gim went over and spoke Chinese to the woman behind the counter, and she brought us lunch for free. I don't know what he said to her, but I'm thinking of learning Chinese myself.

It was the best meal I'd ever had. Have you ever tasted eggplant?

While we ate, we discussed the people and houses we'd seen, but I kept thinking about Mom and Dad. They would have found our note hours ago. I was sure they wouldn't do anything for a while, maybe not until it started to get dark. They wouldn't take our note seriously. They'd think it was a joke.

"What about her?" I motioned to the woman behind the counter. "Let's live with her."

"No," Gim said. "She'd take us back."

The best house to try, we decided, was the one with the grey-haired lady working in the yard. She had actually spoken to us when we walked by and offered us a few peas from her garden.

We waited around in the park until it got close to supper. Saggy missed Mom and Dad a lot and cried into the sock. He said his stomach hurt. Then we went back to the house of the woman we'd chosen and rang her doorbell.

"You again," she said, when she saw us standing on her step. "Can I help you?"

"Yes," Gim said.

She waited for us to say something else, but we

didn't know what to say. Then Saggy started wailing and she told us to come inside.

The house seemed huge, but I know now that that's because I'd lived in a camper my whole life. She brought us to the living room and invited us to sit down. The sofa looked very soft and I felt like lying down on it, I was so tired. She sat on a chair, drew Saggy close and took the sock out of his mouth. (This time he'd put it in himself.)

"Are you lost?" she asked Saggy.

"My tummy hurts," he cried.

"You're probably hungry. Would you like something to eat?"

We all nodded.

She led us into her bright kitchen. It had flowered wallpaper, a big stove and two sinks side by side. She opened the huge fridge, which was stuffed with food, and took out a platter with a pink lump on it. She got a knife out of the drawer and sliced the lump and put the slices on a plate. Then she went back to the fridge and poked around until she found some plastic containers, which she heated up in the microwave. She passed plates around, but before she let us eat, she made us all go to the bathroom to wash our hands.

I whispered to Saggy, "Look. She's got a bath-tub."

"Do you think she'd let us have a bath?" Saggy asked.

"Let's ask."

First we ate. The pink thing turned out to be a ham, but I'd only seen it cut in circles and sealed in plastic in the store. We had carrots and potatoes, and milk to drink. Then she asked us if we wanted dessert.

Saggy and I said "No thanks!" at exactly the same time.

"You're funny kids," she said.

I said, "We really aren't."

She asked if there was anything we'd like instead, and Saggy said, "A bath." She laughed and laughed. I guess we were funny to her, but not to ourselves.

She went to run the tub. When she called us to the bathroom, we saw she hadn't believed us about no dessert. She had filled the tub with some-thing like candy floss. "Go ahead," she said, so I took a handful of the fluff and put it in my mouth.

Uggh! It was worse than rollmops!

She thought this was hilarious, and only after

she had dried her eyes on a towel did she explain it was a kind of soap. It was bubble bath. I guess you knew that.

"I'll give you boys some privacy," she said, and left us there with a stack of clean towels.

It was the first time Saggy and I had ever bathed in a tub. The three of us had so much fun. Gim piled the bubbles on top of his head, covering his bald spot. Saggy grew a white beard. Mrs. Horner (that was her name) called through the door that we should help ourselves to the shampoo. When we finally got out, she said, "Goodness. I thought you'd drowned." She also said to Saggy and me, "You've got red hair! I thought it was brown."

Then she sat us down and asked us questions about who we were and where we'd come from. We had thought of this. We'd made up our story in the restaurant and we stuck to it. "We're brothers," we said. "From Shanghai." We chose Shanghai because Gim said it was an enormous city that no one would ever try to return us to, because it would be impossible to find our parents.

"How did you get here?" she asked.

Saggy blurted, "We took the wrong turn!"

"I've notified the RCMP that you're here with me. In the morning Officer Cowley will come by to talk to you. Tonight you can stay with me."

I felt nervous at the mention of the police. What if Officer Cowley was the grumpy officer from Halo? But Gim said, "All right!"

Mrs. Horner let us watch TV for a half an hour and have a bowl of fresh peas for a snack. She laughed a lot during the program and at one point turned to us and said, "You're very serious children."

Then we had to put on our pyjamas and go to bed, even though it was still light out. At home we never went to bed until the performance was finished. Mrs. Horner brought us to a room that had belonged to her sons. They were grown up now and living in cities. Saggy and I were in one bed, Gim in the other, under matching green and yellow patchwork quilts. I felt like we were snuggled under fields of wheat and flax and canola.

Before she turned out the light, Mrs. Horner said, "The circus has arrived over in Whynot. If you're still here tomorrow night, I'll take you. What do you think about that?"

We kept our mouths shut.

"Good night," she said.

"Good night," we said.

For a long time I lay thinking, first about Mrs. Horner's sons. Were they crazy? Why would they ever want to leave this wonderful house, where they had their own room the size of our whole camper, and a garden they could eat from whenever they wanted? Mrs. Horner was so nice. Didn't they miss her? Saggy and Gim had already fallen asleep and I had no one to talk to. I was alone with my thoughts and Saggy and Gim's snores. Gim made chopping motions with his hands in his sleep.

Mrs. Horner's sons probably didn't appreciate the good life they'd had here. That was why they had left. This made me wonder if maybe I didn't appreciate the life I'd had with Mom and Dad and the Fantastic Flyers before I ran away. I loved Mom and Dad. I loved Grandma Jack and Mr. Fudge and Bruce the Strongish Man. And Mimi and Claude, who called us *chouxfleurs* — which means "cauliflowers," a vegetable we'd never even tasted. And now I started to miss them all.

Please don't tell anyone this . . . I cried.

And then I heard a sound. I sat up in bed. It was dark, so I must have fallen asleep.

"Yip! Yip! Yip!"

The sound was very faint, but getting louder, and soon I heard: "Saaa-ggy! Niii-cky! Saaa-ggy! Niii-cky!"

I got out of bed and crept over to the window and drew back the curtain. There was Coco trotting down the street, yapping. She went right past.

"Saaa-ggy! Niii-cky!"

Mom and Dad appeared in the distance, following after Coco. They must have gone back to the camper after the show and finally decided to believe my note. I was so happy to see them I opened the window to call down. Then I noticed they were wearing their striped socks and big shoes and foam noses and suspenders. It wasn't

Mom and Dad at all. It was Mr. and Ms Toots. Mr. and Ms Toots who wanted us in the circus with them!

"Saaa-ggy! Niii-cky! Saaa-ggy! Niii-cky!" they called into the night.

I watched them clomp past.

I closed the window. It had started to rain. Then I realized it was just me, crying again.

The Mystery Solved

Did you have trouble reading that last chapter? The ink was getting so faint. But this is much clearer now, isn't it? That's because Saggy and I made ink! What you're reading now has been typed with saskatoon berry ink.

Saggy and I went down to the ravine to pick saskatoon berries, which, in case you don't know, are a very delicious kind of berry. I don't know why Saskatoon got to have the berries named after it, when they grow all over the prairies, on both sides of the border. We picked them into rollmop jars and brought them back home hoping to make a pie, except that Mom and Dad don't know how to make pie. They're trying to make normal meals now, but they haven't got to pie yet.

"How about a saskatoon berry sandwich?" Mom suggested.

We tried it. It was actually quite good. I recommend using peanut butter to keep the berries from rolling out of the bread. I also suggest you *don't* use rollmop jars for picking because it makes the berries smell like fish.

After lunch we saw how stained the counter got from making saskatoon berry sandwiches. This gave me the idea to make ink. Saggy and I squashed a bunch of the berries in a big pot with our bare feet. Then I took the ribbon out of the typewriter and threw it in the pot and left it overnight.

Ta da!

Did you think I was typing in blood?

Back to the story.

Early the next morning at Mrs. Horner's, Saggy woke up crying. I figured he missed our parents too, and I didn't dare tell him that they had come looking for us the night before. "It's okay, Saggy," I said. "We'll see them again one day."

Saggy held onto his stomach and curled up in a ball.

"I miss them too," I said, trying not to cry myself.

Gim woke up then, because Saggy really started to bawl. He cried so loudly that Mrs. Horner came into the room and asked what was wrong.

"He's homesick for Shanghai," Gim told her.

Mrs. Horner sat down on the edge of the bed. She was still wearing her pyjamas so it must have been early. "Saggy, what's wrong?"

Saggy just lay there clutching his stomach.

"Does something hurt, Saggy?" Mrs. Horner asked.

"*Wa wa wa!*" Saggy told her.

"Gim? Nicky? I want you to get dressed. We're going to take Saggy to the clinic."

It had never occurred to me that he would be crying for a reason. "What's the matter with him?" I asked.

"I don't know, but I'm afraid it might be his appendix."

Appendix! Grandma Jack had told me about the appendix. It was in the same category as spleens and tonsils. In other words, it might "go."

"Is he going to be all right?" I asked.

"I hope so."

We got dressed as fast as we could. A few minutes later Mrs. Horner came in again, dressed too. She wrapped Saggy in a blanket and carried him out to the car. Gim and I got in the back seat with him. I was so worried about Saggy I couldn't speak. I thought he'd have to have an operation. Mom and Dad would be devastated if they took his appendix out without them. They'd want to be there to cheer him up afterwards.

The clinic was several towns away. Afterward, Mrs. Horner said she was glad it had happened so early in the morning, before there was any traffic on the roads. She'd never driven so fast in her life. "Hang in there, Saggy," she kept calling. When we got there, she left the car in front of the building and, carrying the sobbing bundle of Saggy, hustled us inside. Gim and I had to stay in the waiting room.

Soon Mrs. Horner came back to tell us they were X-raying Saggy's stomach. "Eat some breakfast, boys," she told us, taking two muffins out of her purse. "There's no sense you two suffering as well." For the first time since I was a baby, breakfast wasn't the dreaded rollmops. To tell you the surprising truth, it actually made me sad, but I was too worried to taste much anyway.

A nurse came over and drew Mrs. Horner aside. They whispered for a minute and then Mrs. Horner turned to us and smiled. "Well, Gim. Well, Nicky. I thought it was strange that you weren't excited about going to the circus."

We stared at her.

"Your poor parents are frantic. They called the clinic last night, worried you'd ended up here somehow."

We hung our heads. Then the doctor came in. I knew she was a doctor because she wore a white coat. "You've got to see this," she said, waving for Mrs. Horner to follow. "You too," she said to Gim and me.

We all went into a small dark room where a grey-and-white picture shone on a screen. At first I didn't know why she'd brought us there to watch a show, when my brother was so sick and needed his appendix to go. The doctor pointed at the picture. "What do you suppose this is?"

"That's a tipi," I told her. I'd bought one just like it last year, in Head-Smashed-In Buffalo Jump, and glued it on the camper. Why did the doctor have a picture of it? And the trilobite I'd found in

Drumheller. And lots of other things that looked familiar but that I hadn't seen for a long time: dice, toy castanets, play money, a plastic eyeball, a whistle, a tiny cup and saucer.

"Goodness!" Mrs. Horner exclaimed. "I thought he looked like he needed a square meal!"

Marbles, a rubber snake, a doll, a flashlight, a pearl bracelet. The wooden Easter egg!

Then I understood. We were looking at a picture of the inside of Saggy's stomach.

I don't know how they got those things out of there. Saggy doesn't know either. He missed that part. He says he doesn't even know how they got in. Maybe he slipped out at night and ate them in his sleep.

When Mom and Dad and the Lees arrived at the clinic, Saggy was still sleeping, and Gim and I were in the waiting room with Mrs. Horner. Mr. and Mrs. Lee rushed in, shouting. They sounded angry but they kept hugging and kissing Gim at the same time. I was shocked at the sight of my parents. I'd never seen them sad before. Their clothes didn't suit them any more.

"Mom, Dad," I said. "Don't worry. Saggy's going to be fine. We spent the night with Mrs. Horner. This is Mrs. Horner. She's really nice."

"You must have been worried sick," Mrs. Horner said.

Mom sank down on a chair and opened her arms. I went to her and she hugged me and sobbed. I can't tell you how bad I felt. If you learn anything from this book, I hope it's this: leaving a note is not enough. It's much better to talk things over.

Dad shook Mrs. Horner's hand. No buzz. He'd taken the battery out of his wedding ring. That's how upset he was.

After this tearful reunion, we were allowed to go in and see Saggy. He had woken up and was feeling much, much better. He was so happy to see

Mom and Dad. They couldn't stop hugging and kissing him. (Sorry there's so much kissing in this chapter!)

Dad pulled out a bouquet of daisies that squirted water and put it in the glass by the bed. Mom had brought a jar of rollmops and a box of Pink Pelican Popcorn too, but then the doctor came in and said he shouldn't eat those for a while. She gave my parents a pamphlet. It was called *Canada's Food Guide*.

"Children need proper nutrition," the doctor explained. Apparently Saggy couldn't help eating the gewgaws off the camper. His body was telling him he needed vitamins and minerals. The doctor spoke seriously to Mom and Dad for a long time, and they never made a single joke. Then she said, "I'll leave you alone for a few minutes."

As soon as the doctor left the room, Mom said, "Saggy, Nicky, we're sorry we tried to make you join the circus. We only wanted you to have fun and be happy. We really only want what's best for you."

Dad said, "We're going to leave the circus just as soon as Mr. Fudge can replace us."

Saggy and I looked at each other. It was exactly what we wanted. Then why did we feel so sad?

The doctor returned with a steel tray brimming with gewgaws. "I thought you'd like these back," she said to Saggy.

"Saggy!" Mom exclaimed. "My plastic teeth! I've been looking all over for them!"

Mr. Fudge's Heartbreak

We decided to quit the circus at the end of the summer, before school started, but we didn't know how to tell the others we were leaving. Mr. Fudge was already worried because the Lees went back to the Pink Pearl, their restaurant in Halo. What would happen to the Fantastic Flyers without Mr. and Ms Toots as well? Mr. Fudge would probably go broke. None of us wanted that to happen.

Saggy was soon feeling better, so we invited Mrs. Horner to come to the circus. We had to put on an extra performance to make up for the one that was cancelled the night Saggy spent in the clinic under observation. (Not even Mr. and Ms Toots had felt like having fun that night.) Under observation means someone keeps an eye on you. Mom said they wanted to make sure Saggy didn't have any further stomach trouble, but I suspect they were actually worried he'd sleep-eat something, maybe a stethoscope or a thermometer.

During the show, Saggy and I sat on either side of Mrs. Horner in the front row. When Mr. Toots rode past on his unicycle, he stopped to shake her hand.

BUZZZ!

Mrs. Horner screamed with laughter. Then Mr. Toots squirted Saggy and me with the plastic daisy, but thankfully not Mrs. Horner, who was wearing a nice dress. Ms Toots brought baby Coco over and let Mrs. Horner bottle-feed her. I know Mrs. Horner had a wonderful time because she told me so afterward and she personally thanked Mr. Fudge for giving her a free ticket.

"My pleasure, madam," Mr. Fudge said, with a low bow. When he kissed her hand, a dove flew magically out of the front of her dress.

"Goodness!" Mrs. Horner exclaimed, and she checked inside her dress in case something else was down there. "How enchanting!"

During the show a funny thing happened. Well, lots of funny things happened, but I mean funny curious. I left my seat to go to the bathroom. On the way I passed Grandma Jack in her booth. She was talking to a nicely dressed older woman, telling the story of how she had hatched the chicks. When I came back Grandma Jack was still telling the story, but to a man. I know he was a man. He had a beard. But as I was taking my seat, I glanced over my shoulder and saw her talking to the woman again.

What was going on?

I didn't figure it out until the next day, when I went to get my last package before the summer from the Ministry of Education. Mom had asked me to pick up some rollmops and apples at the store while I was in town. After I'd done my errands, I sat eating one of the apples on the post office steps and there was the woman who had been talking to Grandma Jack, walking along on the opposite side of the street in a skirt and high heels. She stood out, all dressed up like that. When she stopped to look in a store window, her back turned towards me — and I could see that on the other side of her body she was wearing pants and a suit jacket. On the other side she was a man.

Sal-Sally!

I got up and ran. Even before I reached Mr. Fudge's camper I knew he'd already heard the news. "Sal-Sally!" he was crying inside. "Why do you torture me?" I knocked on the door, but he was hollering so loudly I had to invite myself in.

Mr. Fudge was shaking the picture of Sal-Sally and talking to it as if it were alive. "Answer me, woman! Then answer me, man!"

"Mr. Fudge," I said.

He swung around so fast Sir John A. tumbled off his shoulder and scampered under the bed. "Nicky!"

"I saw her," I said. "And him."

"Him!" growled Mr. Fudge. "I'd like to wring his neck. But I can't without wringing hers as well."

I didn't really believe Mr. Fudge would resort to violence. He's a very kind-hearted man. "How did Sal-Sally know you were here?"

"We correspond," said Mr. Fudge. "We've been writing each other for years." He pointed to an envelope lying on the table addressed to Mr.

Fudge, General Delivery. "Every four or five years she manages to escape him."

"Escape who?"

"Sal. Her brother. She escapes him and comes to me."

"How does she escape him?" I asked.

"She hypnotizes him. She learned how from Carlo the Great, back when we all toured together. But Sal wakes up every time!" roared Mr. Fudge. "Sally gets into town and the next day Sal snaps to, and rolls up his sleeve, mad as heck."

"Why does he roll up his sleeve?"

"For a fight. He's a boxer. Well, I'm going to give it to him this time." He jabbed the air feebly. Then he burst into tears.

Sir John A. had come out from under the bed and was trying to climb Mr. Fudge's leg. Mr. Fudge picked up the rabbit and wiped his tears with him.

And I got an idea.

You remember the chapter when I introduced the Lees? Seeing Mr. Fudge's face buried in Sir John A.'s fur reminded me of Mr. Fudge running out of his camper with a shaving cream beard on half his face.

"Mr. Fudge," I told him. "Sal and Sally are

brother and sister, right?"

"Unfortunately."

"I know that if I have something, my brother wants it too. That's only fair, right?"

"What are you saying, Nicky?"

"If you love Sally, someone should love Sal."

"Who could love that bully?"

"You."

"Me?" He was aghast, which, in case you don't know, means shocked and surprised.

I told him my idea. "You have to dress half of yourself up as a woman so that Sal will feel he has a sweetheart too."

"Dress up as half a woman? Not on your life!"

"Why not? If a bear can wear a dress, can't you?" I pointed to the picture of his animal relative in the tutu. The bear looked embarrassed. And so did Mr. Fudge.

He looked at me seriously then and said, "Nicky, I'm going to think about what you're saying."

The next morning Mr. Fudge knocked bashfully on our camper door. "I'll give it a try. What else can I do?"

Everyone pitched in to help our impresario

finally win Sal-Sally. My job was to ride the unicycle to the motel where Sal-Sally was staying
and set up their rendezvous for that evening.

The same man-woman
answered my knock. She
was dressed in half a
silk kimono and he
wore half a velvet
smoking jacket.
"What do you want?"
he snarled.

"Stop it, Sal," she
trilled.

"Mr. Fudge requests
a meeting with you at
seven o'clock in the park,"
I blurted.

"I won't let you go!" Sal boomed.

"I will go!" Sally shrieked, stamping her feath-
ered slipper.

I rode off then. I was afraid they'd start throwing punches at each other, and not play ones, like
Mom and Dad.

When I got back, Mimi and Grandma Jack
were busy sewing together a dress of Mimi's and

one of Mr. Fudge's old suits. Saggy played under the table with Sir John A. while Mom worked on Ms Fudge's make-up. She coloured one eyelid purple. On the same side she applied cherry lipstick. Mr. Fudge had short white hair so Mom couldn't use her pop can curlers.

"I don't know what to do about your hair, Ms Fudge."

Mimi said, "*Grandmère*? Bring some candy floss, *s'il vous plait*."

"Pink or blue?"

"I think pink. It will go better with the dress, *n'est-ce pas*?"

Grandma Jack trundled out to turn on the candy floss machine and whip up a fresh batch. When she returned Mimi arranged it on Ms Fudge's side of the head, attaching it with bobby pins and firming it with hairspray. Then Mom and Mimi and Grandma Jack stepped back to look.

"She's beautiful, Mr. Fudge."

"*Très belle.*"

Mr. Fudge didn't look too happy. He muttered something about being the laughingstock of the circus.

"That's my job, Mr. Fudge!" Mom chirped.

"What do you think, boys?" she asked me and Saggy.

"I think you forgot something," I said.

The women studied Mr.-Ms Fudge, but they didn't see it because it wasn't there.

I cleared my throat.

Then Grandma Jack's rolls began to shake. "Of course!" she laughed. "You need a boob, Mr. Fudge."

Now we all started laughing, except Mr. Fudge.

"Here," said Saggy, and he held up Sir John A. "Perfect!"

Mom undid Ms Fudge's buttons and stuffed the

rabbit inside her dress. We all stepped back again. "It looks natural!" Mom exclaimed. Then Dad and Bruce and Claude joined us outside Mr. Fudge's camper for Ms Fudge's debut. As she emerged, sideways, we all gasped. Mr. Fudge bowed and Ms Fudge curtsied and everyone clapped.

"Uh-oh," Saggy whispered.

The boob was moving. It had migrated down to Ms Fudge's waist. Ms Fudge hefted it back into place, but then it wriggled under her arm and around behind.

"Ms Fudge!" Saggy cried. "Your boob is on your back!"

Now it looked more like a hump, a hump that was kicking. Mr.-Ms Fudge spun around, trying to force the boob to the front again. Half the circus relatives rushed forward to help while Coco yapped jealously around their heels. She wanted to be a boob too!

Yesterday's wash was still on the line, including several pairs of striped socks. If they were all balled together they'd make a good boob, I thought. I ran over and quickly assembled it. Sir John A. was pulled unmagically out of Ms Fudge's dress and replaced with the socks, which looked just fine.

Though we weren't supposed to, Saggy and I went ahead on our unicycles to hide in the park where Sal-Sally and Mr.-Ms Fudge were going to meet. First we pried the diamond ring Dad had got from Pink Pelican Popcorn off the camper and collected flower petals to shower over the happy couple. Maybe they would finally get engaged! We really wanted this to happen because if Mr. Fudge married Sal-Sally he would be happy even if we left the circus.

Sal-Sally was already waiting when we arrived, sitting on a park bench arguing in two voices. We ducked behind a caragana bush and listened to them squabble.

"I forbid you to run away with that awful man!" said the deep voice.

"I love him," said the higher voice.

"Two's company. Three's a crowd."

I was right. Sal was afraid of being left out.

Saggy nudged me. Mr.-Ms Fudge was approaching, taking a big clomping step on the Mr. Fudge side and a tiny teetering step on the high-heeled Ms Fudge side. Sal-Sally stood up, astonished. Sal said, "Who's he bringing with him? Who's *that*?" He said it in an interested way, as though he really wanted to meet Ms Fudge. Saggy and I grinned at each other. The plan was going to work.

Ms Fudge winked at Sal before introducing herself to Sally. "I'm Ms Fudge."

"Pleased to meet you," said Sally, shaking Ms Fudge's hand. "I love your hair. Where do you get it done?"

Ms Fudge patted her candy floss, but she had no chance to answer.

"What are you looking at?" Sal barked, a second before his fist contacted Mr. Fudge's nose.

Mr.-Ms Fudge fell to the ground. Sally screamed, "Mr. Fudge! Oh, Mr. Fudge! I'm sorry! I can't control him!" Saggy and I leaped out from behind the caragana bush and ran to help.

"Let's go," said Sal.

Sally leaned over Mr. Fudge. I'm sure she wanted to help him too, but just then Sal roared, "Now!" and they turned and ran off.

Saggy and I each took an arm. Mr. Fudge sat up. His nose was bleeding. He wiped it on the hem of Ms Fudge's skirt. "That's it," he said. "It's finally over. I'm too old for this."

We walked Mr. Fudge slowly back home. Without a word, he shut himself in his camper. Good thing there wasn't a performance that night.

"What's he doing in there?" we asked Mom.

"He's nursing his wounds."

"His nose?" Saggy asked.

"His heart."

Mom and Dad sat down and in no time they had compiled a list of their best jokes. They asked us to deliver them to Mr. Fudge, but he wouldn't open the door.

"Mr. Fudge? It's just me and Saggy," I called through the window. "Can we come in? We were wondering if you would tell us again about the time Carlo the Great cut you in half." He loved telling that story, especially the part where the half of the box with his legs in it went missing.

No answer. We returned dejectedly to our camper.

Around nine, Mrs. Horner came by with a big basket of vegetables. She'd driven all that way to say goodbye because we were moving on again.

"I also made a saskatoon berry pie," she said.

"I'm sorry," Dad told her. "These kids aren't allowed sweets any more."

(Thankfully, they're not so strict now, because Saggy and I actually like sweets occasionally.) It was a beautiful pie, all golden brown and decorated with fork pricks.

"I understand. Maybe Mr. Fudge would like it. He was so kind to give me a circus ticket."

"Take this to him too." Mom handed Mrs. Horner the jokes.

I don't know why Mr. Fudge answered Mrs. Horner's knock when he wouldn't answer ours. Anyway, he must have liked the jokes because, later, I heard them laughing.

A House for a Dollar

The next day the circus moved on to Douglas, the next town on the list. As usual we were the last camper in the entourage. First came Mr. Fudge's, then Bruce's, then Grandma Jack's (the biggest), then Mimi and Claude's, then Claude driving the truck that hauled the tents and equipment and the sign MR. FUDGE'S FANTASTIC FLYERS, and last, glittering and gewgawed us.

As we drove, we discussed how to break the

news of our leaving to Mr. Fudge.

"I don't want to say goodbye to Mr. Fudge!" Saggy wailed.

"I thought you kids didn't want to travel with the circus any more," Dad said.

"We don't," we said. "But we don't want to say goodbye either. It's too sad."

"Then we won't say goodbye," Mom said. "We'll walk away backwards saying 'Hello, hello, hello.'"

"What an excellent idea," Dad told her, and he leaned over to kiss her.

Mom giggled. "Keep your eyes on that map, mister."

Too late. We were lost again.

Mom slowed down and pulled the camper over. Saggy and I undid our seat belts and joined them up front, where Coco lounged on the dashboard. Through the dusty windshield we saw a vast, cloudless sky, and kilometres and kilometres of butte (see page 78) — the same golden colour as pie crust.

"Where did they go?" Mom asked. "Did I turn? Did anyone notice me turning?"

She shut off the engine.

"Why don't we get out and stretch?" Dad suggested.

After we had stretched it was almost lunchtime, so we decided to have a picnic while we waited to be rescued. Mom put some of the vegetables that Mrs. Horner had brought us into her hat. She tied the tablecloth around Saggy's shoulders like a cape, then we hiked to the top of the butte. Coco raced us and got there first. She always has to be first. As soon as we had the vegetables laid out for the picnic, Mom and Dad shouted "Boo!" and started throwing the food at each other. I hate it when they do that. The tomatoes get all mushy.

"Look," I said. "A house."

We hadn't seen the house from the road, because it was on the other side of the butte — a white, two-storey house with a porch. The upstairs windows looked like surprised eyes and the door, which was painted red, like a mouth. It gave the place a friendly face. We decided that after our picnic we'd drop in on the people who lived there, since they'd probably be dying for visitors, living so far from town.

"We can tell them jokes," Dad said.

"They'll love that," Mom said.

I ate a carrot and a potato. I have to say that raw potatoes are not my favourite vegetable, though Saggy loves them.

Since the house was at the bottom of the hill, we decided to roll down, Coco too; it would be faster than walking. "We roll so well because we eat rollmops," Mom declared. We still eat rollmops for breakfast because, according to *Canada's Food Guide*, they satisfy two essential food groups: Meat and Alternatives, and Vegetables and Fruit.

We rolled down the butte, landing almost against the side of the house. Then we brushed ourselves off and walked around to the front where we saw the sign.

House for sale
$1.00

House for sale
$1.00

"Oh my galoshes! One dollar for this whole house!" Mom exclaimed. "What a bargain!"

We climbed the steps to the porch and knocked on the red front door. Our knock was the only sound.

"It's so quiet," I whispered.

"And peaceful," Mom whispered.

"Maybe no one's home," Dad whispered.

"Why are we whispering?" Saggy whispered, and we all laughed.

Mom and I went to look in the window. "These poor people have no furniture," she said.

"Where do they sit?" Saggy asked.

"On the floor," Dad said. "Or maybe they just stand."

"Don't their legs get tired?"

"I'm sure they must, Saggy," Dad said.

"I'm glad we dropped by, then," Mom said. "They'll really appreciate a joke."

"I don't think anyone lives here," I said. I tried the door. It was unlocked. "Hello? Hello?" I called.

No answer.

We stepped inside, calling, but our hellos and yips sounded hollow. To the right was a large empty room with a fireplace, and straight ahead, another empty room that opened onto an empty kitchen. I'd never been inside such an enormous house. Because the floors were wood and every room empty, our steps sounded especially loud. We tiptoed, in case someone was upstairs. But when we went upstairs, we found four empty bedrooms and a bathroom.

"If this was our house," I said, "this would be my bedroom." I picked it because it had a huge closet with a light and even a window. "I'd put my bed in the closet and use the rest of the room as my study where I'd do my homework and write sonnets."

"What are sonnets?" Mom asked.

I told her.

"A room this big for just fourteen lines?" she asked.

I guess that's why I decided to write something longer.

We looked in the next room. "This would be our bedroom," Mom and Dad agreed. It was the smallest room and the coziest. I think it must have been for a baby at one time because there were pink bunnies stencilled on the wall.

Saggy chose the bathroom.

"You can't use the bathroom for a bedroom," we told him. "There's no room for a bed."

"I want to sleep in the bathtub," he insisted. It was an old-fashioned tub, as big as a boat but with four animal feet, complete with claws.

"But we'll have to keep coming in at all hours of the day and night. There won't be any privacy."

"There's a bathroom downstairs," Saggy pointed out.

We went downstairs to look. When we saw there was a bathtub in that bathroom too, we let Saggy have his way. Besides, this left a bedroom for Coco and a spare room for guests like Mr. Fudge and Grandma Jack and Bruce, when the circus came to town. It was perfect! We stood in the empty kitchen with our eyes closed, imagining it all. But of course it was just a dream. Coco barked because we weren't paying enough attention to her, and this ended our reverie. Still, I took one of the business cards that were stacked neatly on the kitchen counter. They showed a smiling man, a realtor, who, in case you don't know, is a person who sells houses.

When we closed the door behind us, I felt like I was leaving my beloved home for good, which was silly because I'd only been in the house for twenty minutes. I never felt that way when I left the camper.

"The price was right," said Mom as we climbed back up the butte.

"Could you really live here, Red?" Dad asked. "Seriously."

Mom shook her head. "It's in the middle of nowhere. I need people around me."

"We're people," Saggy said.

"But you'd be at school all day. I'd get depressed."

And a depressed clown, in case you've never seen one, is a pathetic sight.

Then I remembered that other time we'd got lost, stuck behind the WIDE LOAD. "We could move the house!" I said. "We could move it into town."

"Moving that house would cost a lot more than the house does. We don't have that kind of money," Dad said.

In fact, we didn't have any money. Neither did we have any idea how we were going to live once we left the circus, but we weren't worried about that. Mom and Dad were confident that we would land on our twelve feet somehow.

"What if there was a way to move the house for free?" I asked.

We reached the top of the butte and looked out over a thousand of Mrs. Horner's patchwork quilts. "Look," Saggy said.

Help had come. Just pulling up was a camper with the world painted on it.

The Strongest Man in the Universe (Almost)

Just yesterday, when I was reading this out to Saggy, he complained that I hadn't really told you enough about Bruce.

"You didn't tell about the time he held the big top down during the tornado."

You know when you go out in a rainstorm and a big gust of wind comes up and turns your umbrella inside out? That was what it looked like, except bigger, of course.

Saggy said, "And you didn't tell about the time he set that train back on the tracks."

It had derailed and was full of screaming passengers. Bruce asked everyone to hold on, then he lifted it gently back on the tracks.

"Or the time he caught that farmer's runaway bull and brought it back."

I can't write everything, can I? The story's almost long enough.

We asked Bruce to come and have a look at the house. Hands on his hips, he circled it, hmming. Then he squatted and rubbed his palms in the dust. He opened and closed his fists and, rolling his massive shoulders, took hold of the corner just above the foundation. He puffed his breath, *POOF, POOF, POOF*, and our hair swirled in his wind and got all messed up.

I should mention that when he held the big top down and when he lifted the train back on the tracks, when he performed all his wondrous feats of superhuman strength, he never actually did it single-handedly. He was never quite strong enough. During the tornado Mom had run out and grabbed the waistband of his leotard. She didn't have to hold on very hard, she said afterward. Good thing; his bottoms might have come down! She said it was harder to hold Coco back. That time with the train? Grandma Jack had given a wheel a tiny nudge, allowing Bruce to get under it and set it on the tracks again.

Now Bruce's face boiled. He roared. His muscles quadrupled as they strained to lift. Finally his huge thighs began to straighten like full-grown trees rising out of the earth. Then they froze, and he looked over his shoulder at me in red-faced dismay. I ran over and hooked the side of the house with my pinkie finger. It tilted like a dollhouse.

"Where do you want it?" Bruce asked.

For the moment, we just wanted to know if he could do it.

The End

After we'd set up the big top in the new town and had our dinner, Mr. Fudge called a meeting as usual. Mom and Dad asked us to come. They were going to have to give notice, now that we had found a place to live, and they wanted our moral support. Saggy and I squeezed into Mr. Fudge's top bunk with Coco, because there wasn't enough room for two extra kids and a chihuahua.

As soon as he had removed his hat and brushed the rabbit pellets off his shoulders, Mr. Fudge opened the meeting by congratulating the Fantastic Flyers on their 11,107th performance. This particular group of performers hadn't put on that many shows, of course, but Mr. Fudge had, over the sixty-two years he'd been in the business. Then he asked if anyone had anything to add to the agenda for that evening. Mom and Dad put up their hands.

"Len, Red," said Mr. Fudge. "Go ahead."

Mom and Dad looked shocked. I think they expected to break the news at the end of the meeting. They blinked at each other, and Mom pulled a polka-dot hankie from her sleeve and honked her nose in it. Dad took it from her and honked his nose in it too, which is kind of disgusting, but that's what clowns are like. They were all choked up. I looked at Saggy. Tears were streaming down his face, just like old times. Good thing he'd brought a sock with him.

"Come on, Red," said Mr. Fudge, impatiently. "Spit it out."

"Ah ah ah," Mom stammered.

"We we we," added Dad.

"It's just . . ." Mom blurted, "we love the circus. We love all of you so much."

"How can we say goodbye?" Dad asked.

Mom turned to him. "I thought we weren't going to say goodbye. I thought we were going to walk away backward saying, 'Hello, hello, hello?'"

"That's still goodbye."

"No, it isn't!"

"Yes, it is!"

Grandma Jack said, "Stop it, you two. I can't understand what you're going on about."

Mr. Fudge broke in. "Let me explain." He looked up at Saggy and me and said, "I guess a couple of little birdies were listening when they shouldn't have been."

I have no idea why he said that to us.

"It is with mixed feelings," Mr. Fudge began, "with great sadness and great joy that I make this announcement tonight. My dearest circus relatives, Mr. Fudge's Fantastic Flyers is in its final season."

The camper filled with gasps.

"As you all know, I'm no longer young. To put it plainly, I'm old. I'm old and tired of travelling. If it had been the age and fatigue alone, I would have stayed on as your manager, and only retired as magician and impresario. However, a wonderful complication has arisen. Dear friends, I am engaged to be married."

Silence.

Everyone staring at Mr. Fudge shared the same thought: Sal-Sally was heartless. Sally had disappointed Mr. Fudge so many times. If she had somehow agreed to marry him, we all knew the marriage would never take place. Sal would drag Sally away from the altar kicking and screaming if he had to.

Mr. Fudge looked around. "What? No congratulations?"

Grandma Jack cleared her throat. "Congratulations," she mumbled, looking at the floor.

Everyone did the same. It wasn't even half-hearted. It was one-eighth-hearted.

"You have all had the pleasure of meeting my future bride, I believe, as she has attended and greatly enjoyed the show."

Someone snorted.

"I know we'll be very happy together. She's a wonderful woman."

No one dared say a thing.

"She's a real woman, that Mrs. Horner."

"Mrs. Horner!" Saggy and I shouted. "Mrs. Horner!" We fell right out of the bunk and landed on Mimi and Claude. Before we knew it, we were thrown back into the air and juggled. The reflexes of acrobats are automatic. "Put us down!" we yelled, but the great roar of happiness over-whelmed our protests. Up and down we were tossed, laughing, while the camper rocked from side to side from all the backslapping.

And the best thing was, we never had to tell anyone we were leaving.

PS: How We Live Now

Bruce put the house on the equipment truck. To lift it, he needed only our encouragement. Saggy and I stayed in the house while Mom and Dad drove the truck. We knew it would be the last time we'd see the country moving outside our windows.

At the very end of Second Street, in Sonnet, Saskatchewan, Canada — that's where Bruce set

us down. Everyone seemed happy to have new-comers, since so many people are leaving these small prairie towns. On one side, Mr. and Ms Frank are our neighbours. They have a very cute baby that Coco is desperately jealous of. She's always sneaking next door and climbing into the carriage, which gives Mr. and Ms Frank a fright when they go to put the baby in. On the other side lives a very extended family of gophers. The view from the window is a geography lesson.

In September, Saggy and I started school. We go by bus to Whynot because there isn't a school in Sonnet. I'm in Grade Five now, so the wonderful Ms Went is my teacher again. I can't begin to tell you how much I'm learning. Every time she opens her mouth, my brain gets bigger!

Owen is in Grade Six, but we see each other at lunch and recess. On the second day of school he presented me with his whole astronaut collection to glue on the camper. And this spring he got the idea to bring his catcher's pads and helmet to school. He wears them when he's practising the unicycle. Then I put them on for tetherball.

Gim is still my best friend. Every Friday, Mom, Dad, Saggy and I drive the camper to Halo and eat at the Pink Pearl with the Lees. Afterward, Gim and I do our homework together and then I try to beat him at Go.

Can you still read this?

After the Fantastic Flyers disbanded, Mimi and Claude went back to Montreal and opened a dress shop. Bruce was hired by a moving company in Saskatoon. He is having no trouble lifting the furniture on his own. Since Saskatoon is not too far away, we still see him now and then. Grandma Jack went to live with her daughter in Nebraska and plans to get started in the poultry business.

Mr. Fudge got married to Mrs. Horner and moved into her house here in Sonnet. He turned his camper into a travelling circus museum that he brings out to the fairs and farmers' markets. Many people come just to see the case of famous eggshells from the chicks Grandma Jack hatched. We run into Mr. and Mrs. Fudge around town all the time and always have dinner there on Sunday nights.

We were just there yesterday, in fact, and a funny thing happened. All of us were in the kitchen with Mrs. Fudge, who was keeping an eye on the pie in the oven. Mr. Fudge nudged Dad and said, "Come on, Len. Let's step outside."

"Don't let him smoke," Mrs. Fudge said to Dad.

"Don't smoke, Mr. Fudge!" Saggy and I begged.

"What are you talking about?" said Mr. Fudge. "I quit. You know that."

He took his wand out of his breast pocket and made Sir John A. appear in Saggy's arms. Then he went out to the garden with Dad.

"Good. Now we can talk," Mrs. Fudge told Mom. She made a funny face and said, "He got a letter."

"Who from?" Mom asked.

"Who do you think?"

Mom gasped. They both looked at Saggy and me, and Mom shooed us out. So we went upstairs to look at our old room again. We think of it as our old room, even though we only slept there one night. It was an important night.

It's Mr. Fudge's study now. All the pictures of his relatives from the olden-days circus are up on the wall. And our pictures are there too: Bruce, Mimi and Claude, Grandma Jack — and us, the Grant family. Sal-Sally, though, is nowhere in sight.

A delicious smell came creeping up the stairs,

so we hurried back down to peek through the oven window. Mrs. Fudge and Mom were chatting in the living room by then. We stopped in the doorway. "I told her he was no longer available," Mrs. Fudge was saying.

Mom noticed us and put her finger to her lips. Mrs. Fudge looked over her shoulder and smiled. "Little pitchers have big ears."

I have no idea why she said that.

"Did Sal-Sally write you back?" I asked.

"Who?" said Mrs. Fudge.

Then *BANG*! The pie exploded!

We rushed to the kitchen. Mrs. Fudge threw open the oven door and waved a tea towel around to clear away the smoke. But there wasn't any. The pie was still snuggled inside the oven, happily browning.

The bang had come from outside.

We found Mr. Fudge out by the garage, sputtering, his white hair sooty, his whole face blackened, a halo of smoke around his head. Dad was rolling on the ground, laughing. We joined him.

Ladies and gentlemen, a caveat! Smoking is bad for you!

I guess you're wondering how we earn enough money to live on. The answer is, we barely do, but with good budgeting and if you grow your own vegetables, you don't really need a lot.

Mom and Dad drove the camper around to all the surrounding towns and put up this notice:

Mr. & Ms Toots!
Clowns for All Occasions

Children's Parties ✿ Adult Parties
Wedding ✿ Funerals

I said that I didn't think anyone would want clowns at a funeral.

"Clowns should always be on hand at funerals," Mom and Dad said. "That's when people most need cheering up."

They actually get quite a few calls.

Next summer Mom wants Dad to paint polka dots on the house. She thinks they would look good on Sonnet's grain elevator too.

Can you still read this, or is it too faint?

As for me, I'm planning on getting this book

published. Then I'll get royalties! So please, if you like this book, buy a copy for a friend. And if you mail it to me and include a stamped, self-addressed envelope, I'll even sign it for you.

In the meantime, we earn a little extra money from our joke stand at the farmers' market every weekend. People like to hear jokes when they're sampling the pickles. Saggy and I help write them so I guess we have more of a sense of humour than we thought. Here are a few examples, for free. If you like them, se d a stamped, self-addr   envelop to Gen   Deliver , Son   t, along with one dollar   the lat st jok s w 'v   up.

Q: Why did the pickl cross th road?

A: To   th rollmops!

Or how about:

A fish was   and put nto a jar. "Hey,   .
What am I   in her with a bunch of pickl s?"
The pic   said, "Don't you

Oh d ar.